WINTER'S GAMBLE

WINTER BLACK SERIES: SEASON TWO
BOOK FOUR

MARY STONE

MARY
STONE
PUBLISHING

This book is dedicated to those who dare to seek love in a world fraught with shadows. May your hearts be brave, your journeys be safe, and your gambles lead to lasting warmth. To the lucky ones who find it, cherish it fiercely. And to those still searching, may fortune smile upon your journey.

DESCRIPTION

Swipe right for love. Swipe left for death.

In the aftermath of another harrowing case, FBI agent turned private investigator Winter Black is battling personal demons: guilt, her grandmother's failing health, a strained alliance with a key detective, and the eerie knowledge that someone has been spying on her family. Amid these trials, Winter's newest case emerges as a rare glimpse of normalcy, offering a seemingly simple investigation far removed from the deadly threats that have marked her recent past.

Until her new client turns up dead, a knife through his heart.

Even though dead men don't pay, Winter feels a deep-seated responsibility to solve the murder of her client. Especially when another victim is murdered in the same manner. The common denominators? Both men were on the Wandering Hearts dating app for people looking to cheat, and the killer's calling card—a gold broken heart charm—was left at the scene of both crimes.

Someone's out for vengeance. And it's personal.

In a bold gamble to catch the killer, Winter and her husband set up fake dating profiles for Winter's office staff, placing them in the crosshairs of a deadly game. But one wrong move could land Winter in trouble with the local police, Noah in hot water with the FBI...and at least one person she cares for exposed to the killer's blade.

The mystery and suspense continue with Winter's Gamble, the shocking fourth book in the Winter Black Season Two series, a stark reminder that the search for romance can quickly turn into a journey through a minefield, where every click might be your last.

1

The ceiling light cast a dim glow over the faded and frayed brick red motel bedspread. Pacing in nervous anticipation, Terry Abbott thought about sitting to wait for his date, but that quilt didn't look like it had seen the inside of a washing machine in months. The room stank of sweat, cigarettes, and sex, and Terry knew he should leave. He should be at home with Nell and Skyler, watching a movie.

Hell, Terry knew he should be doing anything but meeting another woman in the grungiest motel room he'd seen since his college days.

He knew for damn sure his wife Nellie would rather he not engage in this tryst, and he wished he could resist. Just pretend he hadn't dreamed of a night like this for most of his life, even though it meant lying to the one woman who'd ever truly loved him. She thought he was downtown at a new investors' function, celebrating the next start-up about to go public.

And he had been. But after the first twenty minutes at the event, Terry had begged off, claiming the shrimp cocktail hadn't agreed with him. One of his coworkers batted an eye at the obvious fib, but she wouldn't tell anyone he'd left early, least of all Terry's wife. He'd covered for that same coworker a week back when she skipped out on a board meeting to hit the beach with her guy of the month.

It's what people do. We help each other get what we need.

And Terry needed this.

He needed it so bad, it was all he could do to keep his clothes on until his date showed herself.

Surveying the bed again, Terry wondered how much of his skin he'd actually want to expose to any part of the room. Maybe he should flip the comforter wrong side up or hide it in the closet. The Black Cat Motel was hardly his first choice for a night of no-holds-barred fun with no strings attached. People used this venue to roll around, exchange first names or no names, and quietly go their separate ways without a second glance. But at least the rate was cheap.

Nell didn't pay much attention to the household finances, and she surely wouldn't balk at a fifty-dollar cash withdrawal. If she did, he'd just say he used the funds for tips at the upscale hotel hosting the investors' function.

He'd wanted his date to meet him at the nicer hotel hosting the function, since he could've used his corporate card to pay for the room. Even if Nell got nosy about the money, she'd never find that charge.

But Terry's date insisted on the Cat, so here he was, itching for her arrival. He'd left the second key tucked into an empty soda cup from a fast-food joint right outside the door, just like she'd instructed. Any moment now, she'd walk through that door.

He checked his phone for updates. Her last DM read, *ETA 15. Be ready for me, lover boy.*

Oh, Terry was ready. As ready as he'd ever been.

Deciding to take the risk, Terry perched at the foot of the bed, soaking in the beige walls, the stained and torn curtains over the one window, and the ratty, yellowed towels hanging in the little bathroom. *Are they the cause of that funky smell?* He didn't want to know.

He got up and closed the bathroom door.

Terry stayed on his feet, wondering once more if he should just bail. Maybe this was a setup, and a cop or a P.I. would burst into the room with Nell.

The thought had him laughing out loud.

As if she'd be that attentive to what he was doing day-to-day. Since Skyler's birth, Terry's homelife had become one long cycle of routine and dissatisfaction for everyone. He and Nell went to work, Sky went to school, and everyone came home and watched TV after dinner. On the weekends, Nell saw her girlfriends and he saw his buddies, while Sky got lost playing some video game or streaming some show.

Wash, rinse, repeat. Same old, same old for almost a decade.

Sometimes, Terry and Nell would have sex before falling asleep, but she always seemed to need a couple of drinks to get in the mood.

So here he was. Waiting for some chick to show up to this funky place so he could get his rocks off the way he always wanted. It'd be a onetime thing, just to get the urge out of his system.

But, damn, I wish it could be anywhere but this dive.

He'd heard stories about the Cat. A guy who handled Terry's accounts at the office liked to use the place whenever he needed something he couldn't get at home.

Once Terry realized he was in the same boat, well, it hadn't taken long before he was bending that guy's ear for tips on how to set up a one-night stand. He already had profiles on a few dating apps that he kept secret from Nell, but none of them were as good as Wandering Hearts. That app had so many layers of security and could only be reached on the dark web. She'd never find him on there.

Before he'd seen the profiles on that app, Terry had never seriously considered cheating. Sure, he'd scrolled through other dating profiles in search of cute faces and body shots, and he'd watched his share of porn, but Wandering Hearts was so in-your-face, so honest.

The irony of using that word to describe a dating app for cheaters was not lost on him, but that was what Wandering Hearts was. People stated their marital status, their intentions, and their desires plainly, removing all the guesswork.

And, oh, the things he was *finally* going to do. The fantasies his date had promised to make a reality.

He checked his phone again. Still nothing new. If his date didn't show, he'd uninstall the app. He should do that regardless. If Nell ever broke into his phone, that would be the end of everything.

The app was probably loaded with spyware, but what the hell. The DMs from this woman—as well as her photos—were smoking hot.

He thumbed through a few of his favorites while he waited.

A key wiggled in the lock, and Terry backed up a bit to stand near the bathroom door. This was his last chance to call off their rendezvous. No clothes had come off yet, and heck, she wasn't even in the room, just jiggling the doorknob.

He'd had trouble getting his key to work, too, so he wasn't surprised.

Should he just bail? Open the door and say, "Thanks, but no thanks," before slipping past her and fleeing?

Or should he follow through and finally experience a real good time?

Terry leaned against the wall by the bathroom, lifting the

hem of his too-small t-shirt to show off his abs a little. He had a naturally athletic build from a youth spent playing sports.

With one more wiggle of the key, his date opened the door. A shadowy figure stepped inside, closing the door behind her. She wore a wide-brimmed hat and was taller than he'd expected. But, of course, there was no one else in her photos for a reference point.

Plus, most of those pictures were close-ups.

"Hey, I'm Terry."

She hesitated. While the hat obscured most of her face, he could see her full lips, painted with deep red lipstick. Her chin shook a little. Was she nervous too? Or was she already playing her role from the fantasy they'd talked about? Maybe she just needed a little encouragement.

"It's okay if you want to take things slow, you know. I'm in no rush here."

She nodded and inched closer. "I'm glad you beat me here. Did you bring the knife?"

"Yeah, got it right here." Terry patted the hunting knife on his right hip. His dad gave him the blade as a gift for his eighteenth birthday, right before he left for college. He never thought he'd use it for a night of fantasy in a crappy motel room, but he'd asked for a little rough role-playing, and she'd said to bring his favorite weapon to enhance the fantasy. When he'd mentioned the gift, she'd called it perfect.

She stepped forward again, still playing coy, like they'd discussed.

"You're a good man. You keep your promises."

Her voice dropped a little, like she was sure of herself. But she wasn't supposed to start out as the top. That was Terry's role. At least, that was how he remembered the plan from their DMs.

Then she rushed forward, closing the space between

them and bringing her hands to his chest. Apparently, she'd decided to go completely off book, but an officially aroused Terry found her enthusiasm contagious. As she sank to her knees, he let his head fall back against the wall, waiting while her hands went to his belt.

Maybe she was doing what they'd talked about. He was supposed to be holding the knife on her, though. His hand touched the hilt, unsnapping the band that held it in the sheath. He fingered the leather as she undid his buckle. She pushed his hands away, tucking them behind his lower back, before returning to her task.

Terry gave up on playing out the fantasy. He just wanted to roll with finally getting what he'd always wanted from a lover. Closing his eyes, he anticipated her first touch.

His belt came loose, and she slid his pants down his hips. His bare skin turned to goose flesh in the air-conditioned room. Her fingertips traced the waistband of his boxers, hooking in, tugging, and dragging the fabric down to free his dick.

With her hands on his hips, holding him back from thrusting forward, she blew warm, exciting breath across his taut skin.

Her hand slid down his leg as she continued to tease him. When he felt something pulling against his thigh, he cracked his eyes open, tilting his head forward so he could look her in the eyes before she began.

Instead, he discovered her holding the knife in a reverse grip. Before he could react, she swung her hand back and thrust the weapon into his chest.

Agony exploded under Terry's heart. A burning, screaming pain flooded through him, sending him sliding sideways down the wall as he cried out. She went down with him, glaring as she held the knife securely inside him.

"You came here because your heart wants to wander.

Well, now it can, because I'm going to cut it out of your fucking chest."

Terry slipped onto the ugly brown motel carpet. Nell would find him here. She would see him like this and tell Skyler.

He wanted to shout at the woman killing him, to tell her he'd only wanted the fantasy—not to really die. Not to be stabbed with his own knife, which was supposed to be *his* toy for the date, to cut off her clothes.

"Just role…play. Alex, you're…killing me. Why?" Terry choked on his words, coughing up blood.

"I came here to teach your cheating ass a lesson. Liars never get what they deserve, but now they will. And it all starts with you, Terry Abbot."

How does she know my last name…?

Terry yearned for relief, but his arms had gone numb, and with warm blood swimming in his throat, he could no longer speak. The hatred in her eyes told him everything was a lie from the start. She wasn't his date. She was never going to be his fantasy.

She was his end.

He wanted to plead with her, to beg her to stop, to help him stand up so he could go to a hospital. Or home to Nell.

Nellie…baby, I'm sorry.

His killer wrenched her hand from side to side, slicing his insides apart, before sitting back and yanking the knife free. Warm blood spread across his chest and pooled around his body as he rolled onto his stomach.

Terry watched her wipe the blade on the bedspread, adding his lifeblood to all the other indiscretions littering the fabric. She stepped over him, grabbed his shoulder, and rolled him back over. He stared into her malevolent eyes, blinking away tears and trying desperately to lift an arm—to grab at her, pull her hair, *anything*.

He managed only to flap a hand, wet and slick with the blood that had saturated into the mangy carpet.

In response to his lame attempts, a devilish smirk curled the corners of her mouth. She crouched closer, her voice like a whisper in a dream. "Broken hearts are the reason for all the world's pain. If people had more respect for love, nothing bad would ever happen again." She placed something small and cold on his forehead, but he could only focus on the black spots clouding his vision and the fireball erupting in his chest.

Terry's life drained away, soaking into the filthy carpet.

As the light dimmed, his thoughts went to Nellie and Skyler. He feared, even in death, that they'd never love him again. Everyone would know he'd come here to cheat on the family, to go outside his marriage.

And for what?

More tears stung his eyes, and his throat grew tight with the heat of blood and regret over downloading Wandering Hearts and choosing this woman.

He had love, once upon a time. He could have had it again, couldn't he? If he'd tried. For Nellie and Skyler.

Why couldn't I let them be enough?

2

Winter Black-Dalton sat on her back patio, breathing in the late winter air. Though she'd already checked dozens of times, she couldn't stop herself from scanning for any hidden cameras that might be watching her every move.

It'd been nearly a month since she'd found the camera hidden under the eaves of her grandparents' back porch. And though she'd lived in some level of paranoia for most of her life, she found herself checking over her shoulder more than ever now.

Will I ever find peace?

Her laptop sat open on the table behind her, next to an empty coffee mug, her third cup that morning. The weeks since her grandmother's diagnosis of kidney failure had been an emotional and physical roller coaster. She longed to work at her office, but today she needed to stay home and watch over Gramma Beth.

Two mornings each week, Winter had her grandmother over while Grampa Jack ran errands or kept his own medical appointments to deal with his lupus. Even with the worst of

Gramma Beth's health concerns behind them, Winter still worried.

Her grandparents had been the only constant in her life, save for her best and truest friend, Autumn Trent. But ever since Winter left Richmond to relocate to her husband, Noah Dalton's, home state of Texas, even Autumn had begun to occupy a temporary space.

We came here to be closer to family and maybe start one of our own.

The scare with Gramma Beth taught her nothing and no one lasted forever. She couldn't imagine a world without her grandmother, and this recent health crisis had her reevaluating the long hours and devotion to her business. She wished she could change that, but she'd only just gotten her private investigation company off the ground.

Winter checked her phone, anxious for any news from her office assistant, Ariel Joyner. She'd scheduled a meeting with a new client later that day and was itching to return to work once Grampa Jack got home.

Just the thought of being in the office for an entire day tomorrow lifted Winter's mood. It quickly crashed back down when she realized she was looking forward to time away from her grandmother.

Guilt churned the three cups of coffee in her belly. How had her life become a choice between so many demands, all of which she felt a desperate obligation to meet?

She checked her phone one more time before heading back inside.

Still no word from Ariel, and I'm sure Gramma could use some company.

She walked into the cozy kitchen her grandmother had helped decorate, passing through a doorway and the empty dining room—she and Noah hadn't found time to shop for a proper dining table—and into her living room, where a smile spread across her lips and a comforting warmth filled her heart.

Gramma Beth still sat on the sofa, crocheting.

With tightly permed snowy white hair, a round face accentuated by wrinkles, and lively blue eyes, Gramma Beth had been Winter's rock for most of her life. Ever since Douglas Kilroy, the infamous Preacher, had slain her parents.

After the tragedy, Jack and Beth took Winter in, raised her, and tended to the nasty head wound Kilroy had given her. All the surgeries and doctor's appointments had traumatized Winter, but whenever she thought she couldn't take another day of treatment, Beth had been there to hold her up.

"What's that gonna be?" Winter gestured toward the collection of crocheted material in her grandmother's lap.

Beth never missed a beat as she wove the green and yellow yarn into a design. "A scarf for Noah."

Winter chuckled under her breath. "You made him a scarf for Christmas, Gramma. Remember?"

Beth's cool eyes gave Winter a once-over. "That one was gray. This one is more colorful."

Winter didn't bother telling her grandmother that Noah wasn't big on scarves. She knew avid crocheting kept Beth's mind off the endless appointments and treatments for her ailing kidneys.

I'm sure she'd rather be cooking than listening to the smoke alarm go off every time I set foot in front of the stove.

A knock on the front door startled Beth. "That can't be Jack. His doctor's appointment isn't even for another half an hour."

Winter smirked while walking toward the door. "It's not Grampa. He wouldn't knock. It's someone else."

"Who?" Beth asked as Winter opened the door.

Standing on the porch, thumbs hooked into his tool belt, was the grizzled contractor Winter had hired to fix up her office. Kline Hurst wiped his feet on the doormat as he greeted Winter with one of his usual scowls.

She had a soft spot for the ornery guy. On one occasion, he'd saved her life, and he always seemed to be there when she needed him. Still, he'd refused numerous times to attend her family's Sunday dinners, despite the "standing invitation." Since he'd proven obstinate to a fault, Winter decided to step in and ensure her favorite employee and her grandmother finally met.

"Thanks for coming." She waved him inside. "My grandmother's on the sofa."

Kline shuffled through the doorway, his baggy overalls hanging from his slender frame.

As Winter showed Kline in, she watched him assess her sparsely decorated living room. She could only imagine what the older man thought of her decorating skills, especially after he'd spent so much time crafting her office bookcases into works of art. She was grateful she'd at least cleared away some of the packing boxes.

"Gramma, this is Kline. The man I was telling you about who helped me get my office in shape."

A sheepish Kline shifted into Beth's line of sight. "Nice to meet you, Mrs. McAuliff."

Beth lowered her readers from her nose. "Mr. Hurst. I've heard a lot about you." She glanced at Winter. "What brings you here?"

Winter smiled, hoping to sell her grandmother on her idea. "I asked Kline to come and talk to you about the handrails in your shower."

Beth's eyes narrowed. "What handrails?"

Winter added a smidgen of stubbornness to her tone.

"The ones your doctor told you to put in over a month ago. With your go-ahead, Kline wants to measure the area."

Kline nodded. "Yes'm. I know what you need. Installed a few of them in the past. Handy to have when you get older."

"You can't be much *younger* than me."

Winter cringed. This wasn't going well. "Gramma, you have to have them. The doctor said you need them if you get weak in the shower. You're not one hundred percent yet, and I think it's a great idea."

Her grandmother *hmph*ed. "Well, they're not going up in your shower, are they?"

"I promise they'll be aesthetically pleasing." Kline inched toward the sofa. "I know how to make them blend into the shower and bath. You leave all the work to me, and if you're not happy, I can take the rails out or put something else in."

Winter grinned, pleased with her contractor's efforts.

Beth's disgruntled frown slipped, and the right side of her cheek tweaked upward. "I guess you'll need my keys to get inside the house."

Kline hitched up his tool belt. "That's why I'm here. Wanted to see if you had anything specific in mind too."

Beth shook her head and reached for her purse on the side of the sofa. "No. Just don't make it look like I need help walking through my own house. Shower rails are fine, I suppose, but I can get around everywhere else with no trouble. And I plan on taking everything down once I'm recovered."

Kline scratched his chin. "Naturally."

Winter heaved a relieved sigh as her grandmother handed Kline her keys and rattled off the address, along with instructions on where to find her master bath. The way Beth ordered the man about gave Winter hope. It had seemed like forever since her grandmother had shown so much strength.

After the initial diagnosis, she'd spent most of her days sleeping or staring at the TV.

Kline gripped the keys. "Yes'm. I'll see to everything just as you want it." He glanced at Winter. "I'd better get going. Be back in a jiffy with this." He dangled the keys.

Winter showed him to the door, wanting to get out of her grandmother's earshot before she thanked him for coming over. "I found a camera at my grandparents' house about two weeks ago. I want you to sweep for more while you're there. I can't do it because she'd get suspicious."

Kline raised his eyebrows. "What the hell? Why would someone put those there?"

She placed her hand on the doorknob. "To get to me. You know how dangerous this business can be. I've been doing regular sweeps, but two pairs of eyes are better than one."

Once on the porch, Kline stopped and looked over his shoulder at her. "I'll have your back. Don't you worry."

She stood inside the doorway, watching the older man return to his pickup and wondering why she had so much faith in him.

3

Winter's office had never felt so much like a home away from home. When Kline had first arrived to start renovating the interior on that first day, it felt like a construction zone. But now, with the bookshelves complete, the flooring refreshed, and a new coat of paint on the walls, it was like stepping into a space curated specially for her.

Standing on the sidewalk, she savored the sensation before reminding herself she was there to work.

She had a new client to meet who'd been calling for over a week. Because he chose odd hours to reach out, they'd been playing a constant game of phone tag. It was something about a workers' comp claim being challenged. That was all she knew, but she'd be learning more, including his full name, when he arrived later in the afternoon.

Given the intensity of his messages, she and Ariel referred to him as Mr. Down and Desperate.

Ariel greeted her right away as she walked in, jumping up from her desk in a way that sent her brown ringlets bouncing around her shoulders.

"I finally got Mr. Down and Desperate on the phone.

Honestly, just from talking with him, I think you'd find serving court papers more rewarding."

"I appreciate the unsolicited advice." Winter quirked a half smile. "But I didn't start this business to play delivery driver. What'd you learn about our mystery client?"

Ariel, apparently chastened, shifted her attitude from perky to professional. "His name is Ernst Wald. He offered no details about what he wanted to discuss and said he'd like to meet at two o'clock instead of four. So in about twenty minutes."

Briefings at the Bureau were rarely this painful. Harder to bear, true, but still...

Winter pressed a hand to her forehead. "Any chance I could get a mocha?"

Ariel's usual eagerness returned as she beamed. "You betcha, Boss." She hurried to her desk, positioned by the entrance, and put down the notebook she'd been reading from.

The moment her assistant was out the door, Winter made a beeline to Kline. When he'd returned Gramma Beth's keys, he'd reported no cameras around her house. Winter needed to know if any had been found near the office.

Kline had been on his back under the kitchen sink since she'd come in. Even when she gently knocked her boot against his outstretched foot, he didn't budge.

"Got a minute?"

Kline slid out and gazed up at her, his scowl more prominent than before. "What?"

"Any chance you've spotted more cameras here?"

He hauled himself to standing and wiped his hands on a rag that hung from his tool belt. "Inside, you mean? What makes you think we'll find them? How would somebody get in to install them?"

She tucked a loose lock of hair behind her ear, unsure of

just how much she should tell Kline about Justin and his band of merry psychos. "I'm worried someone from my days at the Bureau could be behind this. I helped put a lot of bad actors away, and some of them were real monsters. If people like that want to keep tabs on you, they find a way. Trust me."

"If they're put away, it can't be them spyin' on ya, can it?"

"I'd like to say you're right, but former agents are always paranoid. It goes with the job."

He leaned in closer. "You're not a one-woman army, you know? You got me and the pit bull to help ya."

Winter sighed. "Don't call her that. Ariel's a sweet kid."

"A sweet kid with a pit bull's swagger. And she calls me a grizzly bear, so fair's fair."

Winter watched him lazily push at a rag on the countertop, like his hands just needed something to keep them busy. "Oh, hey, why don't you stop by for dinner on Sunday?" She might as well keep trying to whittle him down.

"Don't seem right, with your grandmother being sick and all."

"She's on the mend, and—"

The front door of her office flew open, causing the bell to jingle like mad.

Winter's hand went to her hip as she spun toward the sound.

A man wearing an ill-fitting suit stood in the doorway, using a cane to support his weight. His waistline fought with the button-down he wore under the blazer, and his hairline had already started climbing back on his brow. Letting the door swing shut behind him, the man adjusted his blazer and patted his forehead as he approached Ariel's desk with a mild limp. The cane took most of his weight on the left side.

Winter stayed beside Kline in the kitchen. "Can I help you?"

The man glanced at Winter but didn't respond. Preparing

herself in case he drew a weapon, she walked across the open office floor to meet him. When they were a few steps apart, he seemed to notice her and paused mid-step.

"Hey. I...sorry, I have a two o'clock with Winter Black."

Seems Mr. D and D has arrived. And he's fifteen minutes early.

"I'm Winter Black. It's a pleasure to meet you, Mr.—"

"I, ah, the matter I came to discuss is confidential. You know?" He peered over her shoulder in Kline's direction.

When she motioned to her office, Wald hobbled forward, maneuvering through the door with his cane leading the way.

Once inside, he leaned against one of Winter's client chairs to take weight off the limb. She closed the office door and took a seat behind her desk, motioning for him to follow her lead.

As he sat down, he got right to the point. "My name's Ernst Wald. My former employer is attempting to defraud me of my insurance claim for workers' compensation."

"You work for Gardner Grocery, is that correct?"

"Yeah. At least, I did. Haven't actually worked since I got hurt, and I doubt I'm still on the payroll."

"Are you saying you were fired over a workplace injury?"

"No, I wasn't fired. I'm being harassed, but...are you sure nobody can hear us in here?"

She waved a finger around at the acoustic panels Kline had installed. "Whatever you say in this office will never leave it unless I later become compelled by a court of law. Or if you're about to admit to a capital crime, in which case you'll want to find yourself a lawyer, not a P.I."

He repositioned himself, fighting to keep his left leg extended. Bending the limb seemed to cause him more pain than walking on it.

"Is this about your leg?"

"It's my knee, but yeah. I need your help getting my

workers' comp claim to keep paying. My boss at Gardner Grocery is trying to intimidate me so I'll drop it. He says I'm faking, but...well, you see how I have to walk."

"Normally, an insurer will hire an investigator, like me, to conduct surveillance of claimants to assist in determining if a claim is fraudulent. Have you noticed anyone following you?"

"No, nothing like that. I expected it, though, with the way Otis is breathing down my neck about this all of a sudden. But my claim's legit. A box of melons landed on my leg and put my knee out of joint three months ago. He saw it happen."

"So why's he saying you're faking? What aren't you telling me?"

Wald fiddled with his blazer, and his mouth pulled into a nervous grin. "I...I'd rather not say. Okay, fine, he sent me an email. The important thing is he's trying to get my insurance payments cut off because he's a cheapskate. But I can't prove it, so I need your help."

Winter sat back. The intensity in his voice spurred a suspicion there was more than a workers' comp claim between the two men. And his reluctance to answer her question raised her hackles.

"If you can't be forthcoming and open with me, Mr. Wald, I can't help you. The investigator-client relationship is based on trust and transparency."

Wald threw his hands in the air. "I'm not the guy you need to investigate. It's Otis Gardner. He's a damn snoop who won't leave me alone. I ran into him while leaving my last doctor's appointment, and then again two days ago outside the clinic where I go for PT."

If his employer was harassing him like that, it could amount to criminal activity, depending on what was said.

"At the very least, he might be facing a Class C

misdemeanor and a five-hundred-dollar fine. But that would be for the courts to decide. Did he say or do anything that you felt was coercive or intimidating? Maybe he communicated a threat in that email. If you showed me the message, I could—"

"I deleted it."

Winter was stunned. "You what? Why would you do that? An email would be documentary evidence of Gardner's behavior."

"I can't...shit. Okay, I got on this app a week ago."

"An app?" Winter wasn't certain she was following where he was going.

"Right. Like a dating app. An app for, um, married or attached people to...meet."

Winter dropped her chin and stared at her desk, counting down from ten. "What does this have to do with your claim case?"

"Well, I went into his office to talk about my case."

"When was this?"

"Last week, on Wednesday. I saw him cruising the very same app on his phone, swiping right all over the damn place. He freaked out when he saw that I'd seen him. I told him not to worry, because I'd checked out the app too. That his secret was safe with me. But then he started going after me for my claim. He told me to call it off, or he'd tell my wife about the app."

Her last case had involved a womanizing embezzler, and if Winter never had to hear the word *affair* again, it would be too soon. "If you're about to ask for help lying to your wife, you can hobble your ass right out of my office."

"No, I swear. It's nothing like that. Nothing happened on the app. It's just a place where you scratch each other's itch, you know?"

"So you're 'talking about' lying to your wife and scratching your 'itch.' Lovely."

"Ms. Black, please. I'm not a cheater. I don't even have a profile on the app anymore. I'm just a guy who got hurt at work, and…I haven't had a win in a long time. But now, Otis is trying to blackmail me…torpedoing my claim…because of that app. Please, I need your help."

Being blackmailed by his employer? That could make this quick and easy. Serving court papers wasn't exactly lucrative, but those gigs came more frequently than the higher paying investigative clients Winter preferred to take on. The recent dry spell, interrupted only by her last and nearly disastrous case for Mat Schultz, made her keen to pick up what work she could.

And it sounds like this one won't involve anybody trying to kill me or my client.

"What's the name of this app you're no longer on?"

"It doesn't matter. It's just the reason I thought my boss got pissed and wanted revenge or whatever."

Winter raised an eyebrow. "The name?"

"I don't know, it was something like Lonely Hearts Club or Wandering Souls. Honestly, I can't remember. Like I said, it's not the point."

Winter didn't buy it, but she was inclined to believe he might be onto something where the workers' comp was concerned. "Okay, Mr. Wald, I'll agree to help you prove that your employer, Otis Gardner, is engaging in illegal intimidation and harassment with the aim of defrauding you of your rightful workers' comp claim. My retainer is eighteen hundred, paid upon completion of the client intake paperwork. If you're prepared to get started, I'll get that ready for you now."

He blanched, startled by the dollar amount, but soon settled into the chair again, nodding. "Okay. Yeah, that's…

that's fair. I knew this wouldn't be cheap, and if it means I get to keep receiving the insurance, it'll be worth it."

Once Winter got the paperwork printed out and went through the details with him, Ernst Wald signed everything and offered to write her a check.

"It'll be easier to use my payment service. I can accept major credit cards or transfer from a debit card linked to a bank account." She held out her phone, showing the app, and lifted a card reader from her desk drawer. With a reluctant sigh, he brought out his wallet and conducted the transaction.

With the ink barely dry on the paperwork, Winter walked him back to the entrance, holding the door open as he limped his way outside.

"Here's my card. Shoot me an email with the times and locations of where you've seen Otis Gardner outside work since this all went sideways."

"Will do. Thank you, Ms. Black."

Watching him make his way to a small white Honda sedan parked down the street, Winter wondered if she were dipping her foot back into the same pool.

Her last case was still fresh in her mind, with all the twists and turns of people unable to remain true to their vows or to the law. Had she just signed on for more of the same?

4

_____

Once free of the irritatingly dodgy man who was also her newest client, Winter leaned against the wall across from Ariel's desk and took a long breath. She stood upright as Kline moseyed his way in her direction.

"You sure you want to take a new case after what happened on the last one? You almost got killed."

"That's not the first time my life's been threatened in the line of duty."

Kline _harrumph_ed. "Wouldn't it be safer to stick with serving summons and stuff, like the pit bull was saying?"

Instead of reminding him, again, how little she liked the nicknames he and Ariel were slinging about, Winter shook her head and stepped around him. Best to leave it alone. The last thing she needed was a civil war between her employees.

"I'll be busy for the next hour at least. Can you finish up that sink today, do you think?"

He grunted but didn't growl as he shuffled his way back into the kitchen.

Just as Winter was walking back into her office, Ariel appeared at the door with two cups of coffee.

Turning, she went over and opened the door before reaching for the mocha her assistant held out to her. "Thanks. Can you get started on a client file for Ernst Wald? I have his paperwork on my desk."

"Sure thing. But…I was going to ask. Is it okay if I leave early today? I have a date tonight. It'll be our second, and he wants to meet at six thirty."

Winter smiled. "And you'll need almost four hours to get ready? Where are you going?"

"There's a new lounge and bar that opened up near the university. It's got all kinds of classic film decor. He's a film studies major and asked if I could play Ilsa to his Rick, but I need to hit the boutiques and find a new white blouse. And maybe a vintage hat."

"You have the hair for it. But, if I remember right, that story didn't really have a happy ending."

Ariel laughed. "We're not role-playing. Just dressing up for fun. The lounge staff call you by your character names. You and Noah should try it sometime. Or we could double! There are so many great movie couples to pick from."

Winter rolled her eyes at the thought of Noah dressing up like a romantic lead. It did sound fun, though. Maybe she'd suggest checking the place out for an anniversary date. "How about you get the Wald file built and call it a day?"

"You got it, Boss. Thanks."

Her assistant headed for Winter's desk and snapped up the Wald documents. Winter followed her in and let Ariel scoot back out before closing her office door.

Mocha in hand, and a good bit of the drink already warming her stomach, Winter fired up her laptop. She started with a more thorough background check on her client.

Satellite-map views of his neighborhood showed average

homes and landscaping. Nothing extravagant, but nothing run-down either. Street views revealed commuter cars in most driveways, a few SUVs and, at the end of the block, a minivan parked next to a neighborhood basketball hoop.

By all appearances, Ernst Wald lived a simple, middle-class life. That didn't preclude him from being a fraudster, of course. Or an adulterer.

Winter ran a Tracers search and pulled up exactly zero criminal activity in the man's thirty-seven years of life. He'd lived in three locations around Austin since moving from the DFW area at the age of eighteen to attend the University of Texas at Austin, where he almost earned a degree in history, before apparently dropping out in his third year to work full time.

A marriage certificate for him and a Patricia Milliken was dated the following year. A birth announcement answered Winter's questions about the sudden end of Ernst Wald's educational career.

"So he's been a workaday dad for close to fifteen years and gets injured, putting him out of work to receive workers' comp payments."

Winter ran a check of the couple's income reporting from the previous tax year. The Walds apparently relied on Ernst as a breadwinner, which matched with his desperation. If his wife couldn't bring in enough and their child was still a dependent minor, the workers' comp payments might be the only thing standing between them and bankruptcy.

Next, she dug into the employer's history, beginning with an investigation of his income reporting for the same period.

Gardner Grocery was a smaller chain, with three stores around the greater Austin area. Income tax reporting showed a company that wasn't exactly raking it in, but Gardner wasn't at risk of going belly-up either.

The chain owner, Otis Gardner, had a twelve-year marriage to his second wife, Bethany Gardner. His first marriage, to a Pamela Dane, had lasted only one year and ended shortly after he opened his chain of grocery stores.

If I'd known P.I. work was going to involve so much infidelity and marital strife...

The sad fact was, Winter *had* known. It was impossible not to hear about what P.I.s routinely dealt with. The television shows all seemed intent on convincing the viewing public that investigators were basically cops without badges, but for every criminal Winter had helped put away, she had dozens more court summons, divorce papers, and surveillance jobs.

Shaking her shoulders and grabbing another sip of her mocha, Winter dove back into the task in front of her.

Otis Gardner's grocery chain had employed Ernst Wald for less than a year, but his employment history showed a ten-year stint somewhere else. Winter put in a call to the company headquarters and eventually spoke to a man in HR.

"Yes, Mr. Wald worked for FarmCo for nearly ten years before resigning."

"Was there a reason given?"

"I'm unable to disclose that information. But I can say he received a stellar recommendation from us on his application to Gardner Grocery."

Winter thanked the man and ended the call. Wald had a long-term employment history and, if that recommendation was anything to go by, a glowing record.

That, coupled with the surface-level view she'd gained of his life, bothered her. Ernst Wald was either already a cheater or teetering on the cusp of infidelity. His presence on a dating app was evidence enough.

Still, his former employer had been "swiping right all over

the damn place" on the same app and was now harassing Wald to drop his workers' comp claim under threat of revealing his activities.

Winter wondered what really transpired between the two men regarding that app.

5

_____

Noah had just finished chopping up an onion and adding it to the pot when Winter walked in from the front room. She took a deep breath. "Smells amazing. What are we having tonight?"

"Tortilla soup. But I got the first course right here, darlin'."

He raced up to her, still carrying his wooden spoon. The brief kiss he planted on her lips earned him a warm laugh. He lingered there, holding her close and delighting in the way they fit together just right. Reluctantly, he broke the embrace and returned to the simmering soup. "Figured I'd make a big batch and bring half to Jack and Beth later."

"They'll love it." She walked to the stove and hovered over the pot, inhaling the fragrant aroma of chicken and spices. "How was your day?"

He shrugged and stirred the pot. "Reviewing case files and looking for leads. You know, the boring office stuff you used to hate."

She stepped back to lean against the counter. "You hated that stuff too."

"Doesn't look like Falkner trusts me enough to give me anything else. I must've gotten under his skin helping you with that last case."

Please don't say it. I know you could've handled it without me. I just couldn't risk losing you again.

He shifted to the cutting board, waiting for Winter to tell him what he knew she had to be thinking. But only the bubbling soup broke the quiet. Noah busied himself by chopping up a small pile of red peppers. "How about you? Anything more exciting than paperwork happen today?"

Winter traced the outline of a vein in the Formica countertop. Bothered by her silence, Noah stopped chopping. "Winter?"

"I'm worried Justin's followers are still out there, watching us. That camera I found at my grandparents' place…I can't stop thinking about it."

"It was just the one, though. Did you find another?"

"No, but I keep waiting for the moment I do. I'm sick of this, Noah. Everywhere I go, I worry there's somebody watching me. Leaving my office. Getting coffee down the street. It's like I can't even breathe sometimes without thinking somebody might be seeing me do it."

Noah set the knife down. Wrapping his arms around Winter's waist, he pulled her in close. She fell against him, her long black hair draped around her face as she nestled into his chest.

"I just want our lives to be normal again. That's all I want. And somebody out there is refusing to let me have it."

His shoulders sagged. "Us, Winter. They're refusing to let *us* have it. What affects you, affects me. It could even be from an old case we worked on. Someone could've followed us from Richmond to get revenge."

She pulled back and tilted her head in question.

He nodded. As much as he hated it, she was probably right. "Or it could be someone else."

"Kilroy's dead, and Justin's in maximum security prison. So who the fuck is doing this?"

"Justin has followers, people who'd do his bidding without even being asked. His incarceration doesn't mean he's less obsessed with you, and that extends to the people who idolize him. You know, I could have our people trace the bounced signal and—"

"I'm doing this without the FBI."

Noah recognized the tension in Winter's voice. She wouldn't budge. He'd have to find a middle ground that would let him stay true to his career without compromising his loyalty and devotion to his wife.

"Okay. No Bureau involvement yet. If we find out Justin's followers are behind this, though, and it looks like we all might really be in danger, I'm going straight to SSA Falkner."

She fumed for a moment, and Noah worried he might've overstepped by laying down the law. But this was his life as well as hers. Her grandparents' lives too. She had to accept he had everyone's safety in mind just as much as she did.

Relief washed through him when her shoulders dropped.

"Okay, that's fair. At the first sign of real danger, you go to Falkner and call in the cavalry. But until then, let me keep looking into who's behind this."

"Let's not take the Justin possibility off the table, okay? And if what you find gets too big for one person…"

She held up her hands in surrender. "I will happily hand over everything I know to the Bureau if it gets too big or has anything to do with my brother or a past case, whether it's one of yours here or something from Richmond."

Noah dug the toe of his cowboy boot into a gouge on the stone floor. "Do I have your word on that?" He tilted his head as he gazed at her, the slightest hint of a grin on his lips.

"Keep looking at me like that, and SSA Falkner can set up incident command in our backyard."

Noah gave her another kiss, then picked up his knife and got back to cutting. "I'm gonna hold you to that. But seriously, how often are you sweeping your office and the houses?"

"Daily. I checked our porch before coming in. It's clean. Kline's doing the office for me."

He cocked an eyebrow. "Kline? So he knows?"

She went to his side and put her arm around him. "He's in our corner. We can trust him."

Noah shook his head. "I never doubted his integrity, and he sure seems devoted to you. You ever consider this could be related to a new case? Maybe someone's hired you under false pretenses." Noah scooped up a handful of the chopped red peppers and carried them to the pot.

Winter rested her hip against the counter. "I doubt it. All I've taken on lately are divorce cases and background investigations. Nothing earth-shattering."

"What's the latest case you picked up?"

"It's either workplace harassment and intimidation or disability fraud. A small business owner thinks an ex-employee is using a fake injury to rip off the company. The employee is my client, who insists his former boss is intimidating him into dropping the claim. There's an as-yet-unnamed app involved, which both men had profiles on. He caught his boss on it."

"I can guess what kind of app that is. Am I warm or cold there?"

"Four-alarm-fire hot. According to my client, the people on it 'scratch each other's itch.' That's what I have so far. He also denied remembering the name, but he did say something about lonely hearts or wandering souls or some crap."

"Sounds like something's wandering. Not so sure it's his soul."

"My sentiments exactly."

"And you've learned enough that you can rule out fraud and focus on the intimidation angle. Or am I giving my wife too much credit for being good at her job?"

She smiled. "Nothing I've found indicates the employee is a fraud. Long-term employment history and a glowing recommendation from the previous employer."

"What about the injury?"

"Need to do more legwork. I was going to start with a stakeout tonight."

"Is that a good idea, considering somebody's already staking *you* out?" Noah frowned. "You should stay home and play it safe."

"Since when have I played it safe? It's just a simple stakeout in a nice neighborhood."

He stopped stirring his soup. "Where? And define 'nice' for me, please."

She twisted her lips and raised an eyebrow. "Nice, as in, basic mid-century construction that's been kept in good repair. Mostly middle-class, working families. No HOA that I'm aware of, but the lawns all look mowed, and none of the driveways have cars up on blocks."

"The address, Winter. I need to know where you're going in case something happens."

"It's just a few blocks from my office, over on Cresper Drive. I'll text you the address."

Every bone in Noah's body told him to wrap his arms around her and never let go, but he knew better than to insist she accept his protective nature. He nodded and went back to his soup, giving it a stir. "Okay, so you'll just grab a few pictures, see if there's any indication the injury was faked. That's it, right?"

She stepped up behind him and put her arms around his midsection, resting her head on his back. "I'll be away for two or three hours at most, and then I'll come right home."

Noah sampled the soup, dashed in a touch more seasoning, and lowered the heat. He settled his arms over hers. "I always hated stakeouts."

"First, you hate reviewing case files, and now you hate stakeouts? Noah, how much Bureau work is left for you to love?"

Within her embrace, he turned around and brushed a strand of her hair off her forehead. "I don't hate all stakeouts. I actually enjoyed them quite a lot when they were with you. We always had fun together."

Winter squeezed him and gave him a kiss before pulling free. She went to a cabinet above the sink and grabbed a couple of soup bowls. "I wish we could still work together."

"Maybe one day we can revisit that idea."

She glanced at him. "Working together for my agency or as agents? Because I'm done with the Bureau, and I thought you loved being an agent."

"I do, but you never know. Things can change." Noah couldn't hide his surprise at his own words. He stared at the floor for a moment, mulling over what he'd just said.

Winter set the soup bowls on the counter and brought her hands to his shoulders. "Hey, Dalton. You still in there?"

"Yeah, I'm here. Just…I guess you're not the only one in this family holding something close to your chest." He'd never felt unhappy at the Bureau. Frustrated, sure, but nothing about the job had bothered him enough to consider a career change.

Winter looked him in the eye. "We got here together, and we'll keep going together. If something at work is making you think twice about being an agent, let me know. Okay?"

"You know I will. But right now, we should think about

eating so we can get that soup over to Beth and Jack. It smells about done."

While Winter busied herself with the bowls and spoons on the counter, Noah readied a leftovers container for Winter's grandparents. Thinking of them had him remembering the night Beth's kidney failure made itself known. They'd been gathered in her kitchen, waiting for her Sunday dinner to come out of the oven. And she'd simply collapsed.

Noah looked at Winter, seeing the weight of worry holding her shoulders down. He thought about the camera she'd found, and that put his teeth on edge.

Someone was watching them. Noah's focus had to remain on ensuring their safety in every way possible.

6

A swarm of police cars and uniformed officers crowded her client's driveway on Cresper Drive and the surrounding sidewalks on both sides of the road.

The evening air cut through Winter's jacket as she got out of her vehicle, walked over, and stood in front of the Wald family home. She'd intended to park across the street and watch the home from the privacy and comfort of her Honda Pilot. So much for that. With flashing blue-and-red lights reflecting from every window, the whole neighborhood had to be alerted by now.

A simple burglary couldn't justify this many cops and vehicles, and that much crime scene tape couldn't mean a simple burglary had occurred. Winter knew in her heart that her client was no longer alive. Someone had entered his home and killed him. Possibly his wife as well.

The largest window in the house overlooked a rose garden beside the front door. Bright light shined out from the front room lamps, revealing at least four people walking around inside.

Winter pulled her jacket closer as she approached the

small crowd outside the cordon of yellow tape. A few neighbors, gathered on the sidewalk, stared in shock at the unfolding scene.

She settled in next to a woman in a pink bathrobe. "What's going on?"

"Someone killed Ernst. I can't believe it. I just saw him this morning. I keep asking if Patricia's inside, but no one will tell me anything." She faced Winter, tears in her eyes. "Do you know if Patricia was home? I can't understand why anyone would hurt them."

Winter pitied the bereaved woman, who seemed to feel the Walds were closer to family than neighbors. "I'll find out." She patted the woman's arm and headed straight for the officer positioned on the other side of the yellow tape.

"Excuse me, what's going on?" She motioned to the house. "Ernst Wald is a client of mine. I was supposed to meet him here tonight."

The officer—white and dressed in street blues bearing a name tag identifying him as *Carlyle*—gave her a once-over. "And you are...?"

She retrieved her ID from her jacket pocket. "Winter Black. I'm with Black Investigations." She held her breath, hoping her name hadn't hit the cop's ears like a bad omen. On her last case, she'd earned a reputation around the Austin PD.

He tipped his head as if considering her credentials. "Wait here."

Carlyle paced across the grass to the home and disappeared inside.

Winter waited, her palms itching. This wasn't good. She'd come to ensure her newest client wasn't really engaging in insurance fraud, and now he was dead. Coincidence? Winter didn't believe in coincidences.

Carlyle soon emerged from the home, accompanied by a Black man in a brown suit and yellow tie.

Winter smiled, glad to see a familiar face. Darnell Davenport didn't return the gesture.

Carlyle stopped in front of her, hands on his hips and a quirk to his mouth. "You want to tell the detective and me what you're doing here?"

"Give it a rest, Carlyle." Darnell gestured toward the house. "Let me talk to her alone."

He waited for the junior officer to leave before he glared at Winter, his dark eyes brimming with anger. "Again?"

"It's not like that. I was here to do surveillance on the guy. He was a client."

Darnell laughed out loud. "You're doing surveillance on your own clients now? Remind me never to hire you."

She rolled her eyes but grinned. "I was just ruling a few things out before going any further with his case."

Darnell stared at Winter, all humor now absent from his voice. "Why is it every homicide in my city has you behind it?"

Winter scoffed. "I didn't kill him. You know that."

"Do I? Where were you between the hours of six and nine this evening?"

Lifting an eyebrow, Winter barely choked back a laugh. "I was at home with my husband, having dinner. We then went to my grandparents' house for an hour. I literally just drove up the street to begin my stakeout of Ernst Wald, checking for a limp."

Darnell raised his hands, chuckling in surrender. "I'm sure that all checks out, and Special Agent Dalton won't have any trouble corroborating for you. So tell me what you know about the dead guy."

She eyed the house. "Tell me what happened, and I'll share what I know."

Darnell put his hand on his hip. "Someone put a knife in the victim's heart."

That was a surprise. "My client's heart. He was alone?"

"Uh-huh. Wife's out of town. What kind of client was he?"

Winter shook her head, forcing herself to focus on the question. "Possibly involved in insurance fraud or being intimidated by an employer who was."

"Sounds serious enough. Anything give you the idea your new case might lead to murder?"

"I don't know." She pressed the heel of her hand to her eye, still unable to believe this was happening. "That was part of my plan tonight, to check on Wald and see if his injury claim matched up. He limped well enough in my office."

"But you hadn't seen him on his home turf yet, where he might have dropped the act. If it was an act."

She nodded. "That's about the size of things, yeah. Any defensive wounds? Upturned furniture, signs of a struggle?"

Darnell shook his head. "No, but there was a dinner set for two."

"Dammit. I knew he was full of shit."

"Come again? First, he's involved in insurance fraud. Now it sounds like you had something else on the man."

Winter took a deep breath, giving herself a moment to decide how much to share. "He and his employer were both active on some dating app. The employer started harassing Wald about his workers' comp claim after he caught him perusing profiles. Like the boss got spooked that Wald was about to blow his cover."

"Okay, and you're thinking he was? Help me out here. I'm not seeing the link."

"I told him to get lost when he mentioned adultery, and he promised he wasn't on the app anymore."

"The guy was desperate not to lose his insurance payments, but you're telling me he was ready for date night?"

Darnell huffed. "Two filled wine glasses…good stuff from California too. Seared scallops on the stove. Two slices of chocolate mousse in the fridge."

"And his wife's out of town." Her nails bit into her palms. "The son of a bitch lied to me."

Darnell went around to her side and glanced back at the house. "Even had candles burning in the bedroom."

The lying, cheating sack of…

She took another deep breath. "I guess it's too much to ask that catching Maggie Reynolds would bring an end to unfaithful spouses across the great state of Texas."

Her last lucrative case had involved a serial cheater and his bevy of conquests, which happened to include two women with a long-standing rivalry. One of them, Maggie Reynolds, had transformed that conflict into a murderous quest for revenge.

"You have anything on the unsub?"

"We didn't find any footprints leaving the home. There's a pool out back. No signs of blood on the patio or in the water. The gate along the security fence, leading to a back alley, was closed and locked. Nothing there either. With the amount of blood around the victim… getting away like that, leaving no trace…that was quite a feat."

She noted the deepening worry lines around Darnell's mouth. "So you have nothing at all?"

He dropped his head and adjusted his tie. "How do you feel about coming downtown to answer some more questions for me?"

Winter's stomach shrank. "You're kidding."

"I wish, but I got a body and a private investigator who shows up on the scene to do surveillance on my dead guy. No matter how much I'd love to send you home to your FBI man, the department has to clear you. You can tell me more about the beef between Wald and his boss and that app you mentioned."

She checked the surrounding street. Was Ernst Wald's murderer among the faces peering back at her from the sidewalk? Training had taught her that killers frequently returned to the crime scene. It was an unavoidable urge for them, to see the results of their handiwork or gauge how well they covered their tracks.

They're here. I can feel it.

Two doors down, a sedan pulled into a driveway. A couple dressed for dinner emerged, mouths gaping at the scene before them.

But Winter didn't catch any red glows or feel the signs of an oncoming vision. None of the faces in the crowd registered as any more shocked or surprised than the rest, and nobody smirked as if pleased by what was playing out on their street.

"I need to call Noah. He can meet me at the station."

"Go ahead. I'll follow you over there, and we'll make it as quick as we can." After he stepped away to his car, Winter retrieved her phone from her jacket pocket. Noah answered on the first ring.

"What's up, darlin'? You okay?"

"I need you to meet me at the Austin police headquarters." She waited as Darnell wheeled his vehicle around beside her Honda Pilot. "I might've gotten myself into a situation."

Noah paused just long enough that Winter wondered if he'd fallen asleep. "What kind of situation?"

Winter sighed. "Remember that stakeout I was going to do tonight? Well, my client was murdered, and I'm going in for an interview."

The distant wail of sirens carried through the open window.

"What the hell?" Noah's shout carried through her phone speaker.

Winter ran her hand across her forehead. "Just get there as fast as you can. Darnell isn't happy that I keep showing up whenever a body drops on his streets."

Winter plopped into the chair across from Darnell in the cold Austin PD interview room. He slid a paper cup of coffee across the table to her.

"You look like you could use this."

She wrapped her hands around the cup, eager for some warmth. "What is this? I know interviews aren't fun for anyone, but you have to get answers. I already told you everything I know about Ernst Wald and his boss. Twice. What aren't you telling me?"

Darnell leaned against the table. "Do you know a man named Terry Abbott?"

She shook her head before sipping the bitter coffee. "No. But since you're asking me, I can take a guess. Terry Abbott was murdered, right? Fancy dinner for two, wine and candles again?"

"Not even close, except for the murdered part. He was found at the Black Cat Motel early this morning. Similarities to how your man Ernst Wald died make us think the two are connected."

"Similarities?"

"Stabbed in the chest, with roughly the same size wound, so we're thinking same blade. The M.E. hasn't confirmed, but it's close." He reached into a folder he'd brought with him and drew out a pair of evidence bags that he set between them.

Each bag contained a small gold item.

Winter hunched forward to examine them. "Gold hearts. Each with a crack etched down the middle, like they're supposed to be broken. I'm guessing these are from the crime scenes?"

Darnell nodded. "Placed on the foreheads of Terry Abbott and Ernst Wald after they'd been stabbed through the heart. Purposefully staged."

"A killer's calling card. Great. But what puts these men together in a killer's mind?"

Darnell grimaced. "Million-dollar question right there. I was listening when you told me about Wald and his boss. Sounds pretty mundane, but we'll look into it. Tell me about this app, though."

Winter gave him the rundown based on what Ernst Wald had told her. "He never named it specifically. Something about hearts." She cast an eye at the charms in the evidence bags. Hearts were certainly showing up a lot at the moment. "Did you find his phone, or Abbott's?"

"Neither was found with a phone present. We're still following up with the spouses, checking their vehicles and, for Abbott, his place of business."

"What did he do?"

"Executive with a financial firm…one of these venture capital outfits that play the angel investor game, but they're really in it for the dividends. Married, as you know. The couple had one child. A daughter. We assume he went to the Black Cat to meet someone. He told his wife, Nellie Abbott, he was at an investors' function downtown. While that checked out, people there say he left the event early."

The wheels in Winter's head began to spin. "And Wald's wife, Patricia, was out of town while he was cooking dinner and drinking wine with someone else."

"Now you see why I brought you here."

"Because you know I'll help you catch this killer?"

He pushed her purse and wallet back to her, shook his head, and stood up. "Bring me whatever you can dig up, but try to stay clear of any crime scenes."

She followed him to the door. "Why don't you let me see what I can find out about Abbott and Wald?"

"Good place to start. In fact, I'm already doing that." Darnell opened the door, grinning at her.

She smiled back, laughing as she stepped into the hall. The hum of ringing phones and buzzing conversation filled her ears. Winter didn't hear someone slip in next to her, but when arms enveloped her, she recognized Noah's warm, sweet scent.

"You okay?" His lips brushed her temple.

She wrapped an arm around his waist. "Fine."

Darnell stepped closer. "Get her out of here and keep an eye on her. She's trouble."

Noah frowned at the detective. "Don't I know it." He ushered her down the hallway, his arm tightly wrapped around her waist. "What did they ask you?"

Winter eyed the officers clogging the hall, carrying folders and tablets and seemingly preoccupied with their cases.

"There's another victim. Terry Abbott. He was killed in the same style as Wald." She stepped through the glass door leading to the precinct's intake area, relieved to escape the noise in the hallway. She waited for Noah to join her.

"What style?"

"Both men were engaging in unethical activities when they were stabbed in the heart, possibly with the same weapon. Abbott was married and told his wife he was at a business event. He was, but left early, and was later found dead at a motel. Wald was cooking a fancy dinner for someone at his place while his wife was out of town."

"I'm guessing Darnell's already talked to the wives and secured alibis, but that doesn't rule out a third party they could've sought help from."

"How many suburban housewives know who to call when they want to take out an unfaithful spouse?"

Noah hesitated at the door that led to the street. "It scares me that the answer might be more than you or I think. It's not like you haven't walked these streets before. The Electrocutioner made a spectacle out of killing, but plenty of other people would opt for a simpler method. Like a hired pro with a knife."

Though he had a point, it didn't feel right to Winter. "I seriously doubt these were professional hits. Do you think the Bureau has their eye on this yet?"

When he opened the door, the cool air added to the chill plaguing her. She breathed in a faint sulfur smell brought in by the south winds from the oil fields. Stepping onto the sidewalk, she hugged her jacket closer.

Noah set his hand on the curve of her back. "I can do a little digging. I review all the homicides that local PD's working, looking for links to any cases we have on file."

Pride and satisfaction surged through Winter. Noah was one of the best agents she'd ever worked with, and his powers of observation never ceased to amaze her. He could pick up on any subtle details in a case that might link the murders. He'd done so on her last case and had helped her stop a killer.

Maybe working together could be in the cards.

"I knew I married you for a reason, Agent Dalton."

Noah smiled, but the gesture didn't last long before his face went slack. "Could any of this be a coincidence?"

"I doubt it. Darnell probably didn't tell me everything. He started off with the 'similarities' line, but eventually said both men died from stab wounds to the chest. And we know they were both involved in some kind of infidelity at the times of their deaths. Oh, and calling cards were left at the scenes in the shape of tiny gold broken heart charms."

Noah ran his hand through his hair. "Similar M.O. and circumstances could mean the same murderer."

She hugged him tighter as they walked to the garage entrance next to the station. "Maybe Wald and Abbott were marked for some other reason. They owed money or pissed off the wrong gangbanger at a stop light."

"But how does that explain Abbott being at a dive motel and Wald cooking dinner for a guest who never showed or didn't leave a trace if they did? You ask me, the possible adultery angle is the clearest link."

Once they reached his truck, Winter hooked Noah's arm in hers and leaned in for a kiss.

Noah pulled back and studied her face for a moment. "Oh, no. I know that look. You're going to charge into a murder case hoping to solve it. Don't you have enough to deal with at home? A dead client isn't going to pay you. Beth is still on the mend."

She squeezed his hand. "I just want to do a little digging, maybe help the PD out. He was my client. It's my responsibility."

Noah ran his thumb along her chin. "If I didn't agree, would that stop you from doing whatever's boiling up in your mind right now?"

Um, probably not.

She shrugged. "No, but you want me to use you as my

backup whenever I'm about to get into trouble. So back me up here."

Noah's green eyes practically glowed with worry as he appraised her. "Keep your eyes and ears open and keep me posted. And no heroics."

Winter smiled, warmed by his concern. "I can start with my client's old boss. Otis Gardner. I'll stop by the grocery warehouse where Wald worked."

"Sounds safe enough." Noah nodded to the garage entrance. "But watch your back and make sure whoever did this doesn't discover you're after them. I don't want anything happening to my teammate, okay?"

"You got it, Dalton. Care to watch my back on a drive past Ernst Wald's home? I want to give the neighborhood a look while this is all fresh in my mind."

"Might as well. It's not like I'll be able to sleep anytime soon."

A police siren in the distance sent a shiver through Winter. She didn't want to think anything could go wrong, but she knew better than to expect the best while investigating a murder.

Hope for the best and prepare for the worst.

8

I sat in my parked car down the block from Ernst's home with my rideshare app open as if I were waiting for a fare. Ernst's body was being wheeled out of his home on a gurney. I grinned as two cops exited the home behind the EMTs. The lights remained on inside. With two patrol cars parked down there, they were probably leaving a team of officers to guard the property.

Or maybe they weren't done searching the house for clues.

Good luck. You're going to need it.

Where Ernst's blood soaked into my blouse, the fabric clung to my skin, all wet and clammy. I snugged my jacket tighter around me. None of the cops had noticed me down here yet, but I'd only pulled up twenty minutes ago, and I was keeping them pretty busy.

Slipping out Ernst's back gate had been easy enough. He'd even done as I'd asked and left a copy of the key under a rock for me, making it simple to get in when I arrived and to leave as though I'd never been there.

Cheaters like him are so easy to manipulate. It's almost like he wanted to get caught.

After killing Ernst and getting back to my car, I'd driven around Austin for a few hours, stopping outside of restaurants and bars, exactly at the locations my rideshare app had directed me to for pickups.

It helped having proxies set up to call in for rides, providing me a rock-solid alibi should the cops ever find me. True, I lacked proof that I wasn't near Ernst's house when he was killed. But I did have a fake ride arranged for a house two streets away, where I'd parked before walking to Ernst's back gate and letting myself into his yard.

From what I could tell, the cops had canvassed the area well. Dressed in robes and nightclothes, as if they'd been roused from sleep, a few neighbors lingered on their front walks.

And how true that was. Killing Ernst might just be the wake-up call these people needed to know that cheating and infidelity came with consequences.

I watched as the ambulance and cops drove away. The last few onlookers ambled up their walks, pulling robes around their bodies and shaking their heads. Like deception and murder were intruders in their quiet little neighborhood.

I knew better. Ernst wasn't the only one around here who'd downloaded and started using my app days after it launched, but I couldn't very well pick my next target from the same neighborhood.

Ernst's phone would soon be safely tucked away at home, along with Terry's. I'd taken a risk keeping that evidence, and I'd have to destroy both devices at some point, but leaving them behind would've been worse. The cops would break into the phones eventually and uncover the network of paths Terry and Ernst had taken.

Paths that led them to the center of my web, where all cheaters and liars met their end.

Opening Terry's phone had been easy enough. The spyware he had unwittingly installed when he downloaded my app gave me his keystroke data. His password had been the lamest one I'd ever seen.

I don't know what I expected from him, but *MasterAbb0tt69* made me throw up in my mouth a little.

His wife's text was straight and to the point.

I know you're not at the dinner. So where R U?! I'm giving you one more chance before I call a detective, and she'll find the truth.

Poor Nell Abbott. So delusional, giving her husband one more chance. She obviously knew he was a cheater.

My mouth curled into a satisfied smile when I thought about all the trouble and money I'd saved her.

Divorce was so expensive and so stressful.

And she'd probably been right. It hadn't taken much googling before I found three P.I.s with offices near the Abbotts' home address.

Only one of those P.I.s was a woman.

Winter Black-Dalton, formerly of the Richmond, Virginia Violent Crime Unit.

Her beauty reminded me so much of my ex-girlfriend, Dani. If I were to remain successful and free to move about, I'd need to avoid attracting Winter's attention. That meant none of my future targets could be linked to her in any way.

I opened my app and scanned for the latest users to download it. The numbers made my head spin. So many people willing to explore a life of lies and deception. They had no idea what they were throwing away.

Commitment meant so little to people nowadays. Nobody even bothered to consider the weight of the promise "to have and to hold." I'd been scarred by a loved one's failure to uphold vows. I knew the pain of being lied to. Cheated on. Robbed.

Nobody I'd ever given my heart to had returned my love in kind, much less in full.

People always left a back door open, some way to sneak out the minute things got difficult. And who was left picking up the pieces but the one who was fully committed from the start?

Me. I'm the one who always had to clean up the mess. Sweep up the remains and sift out what was worth holding onto from what belonged in the trash.

After my last relationship ended with my lover departing for what he no doubt thought of as greener pastures, I vowed I would never again be taken for granted.

And I vowed to ensure cheaters didn't get away with their crimes.

Scrolling through the usernames on my app, I realized just how big a task I'd set for myself. Close to ten thousand Austin-based users had downloaded Wandering Hearts since I launched it last week, with nearly seventy percent of those users active every day.

That much activity in such a small geographic area wouldn't go unnoticed. Still, I had the app hosted on a secure server, which could only be accessed through the Tor network, and my VPN connections ensured I couldn't be found—at least not without devoting significant resources to the task.

It wasn't like I was selling illegal services or products. It was a dating app, like any of the others out there.

But if a former FBI agent starts snooping around, I might need to shut down the app entirely.

Then how would I find the cheaters who needed to be taught a lesson? How would I ensure people learned to value love by seeing the consequences of treating it like garbage?

Heart in my throat, I scrolled rapidly through the usernames, collecting the first four to catch my eye. I was choosing at random, yes, and hastily. But I'd still make a point of showing the world that cheaters didn't succeed or survive.

After saving the names I'd found, I closed out of all my apps and shut down my phone. As I plucked my keys from the cupholder, the bright glare of headlights shined into my car. I fumbled my keys to the floor, reflexively ducking down below the dash.

Had the cops zeroed in on me after all?

They couldn't have any reason to suspect me. I'd removed my jacket when Ernst let me in. And used it to contain his blood on my top and arms on the way out. My wig kept my hair neatly contained so I wouldn't leave any DNA behind. I'd thrown the evidence into a dumpster behind one of the bars I'd gone to earlier.

The cops couldn't know I'd been the one to pierce Ernst's cheating heart and leave my little charm on his forehead. I did everything tonight just as I'd done with Terry.

I reached one hand between my feet to collect my keys and slowly sat back up.

A heavy truck engine rumbled past me. In my side view mirror, I watched the vehicle park in front of Ernst's house, followed by a Honda Pilot. A woman climbed out of the SUV and shuffled over to the driver's side of the truck.

That long dark hair reflecting the glow from the streetlight above belonged to Winter Black, the P.I. Terry Abbott's wife had planned to call.

The former FBI agent.

Shit.

I couldn't start my car now, not with her and that other driver right there not even a block from where I sat.

Winter's silky hair and shapely figure mesmerized me as

she stood next to the truck, chatting with the driver. Boyfriend? Husband? The connection appeared somehow romantic. I could tell from her body language.

Down the street, my ex-girlfriend's doppelgänger lingered before Ernst's home, staring. A few minutes later, she returned to her Honda and got in. She made a U-turn and drove by me. The truck used a driveway to reverse before following Winter into the night.

Ah, love. But if Winter's body language was anything to go by, the poor driver was destined to find out his significant other's definitions for love and commitment were different than his.

I'd awakened from my love stupor a while ago. After my last boyfriend, Simon Chen, used me and stole everything— my creation, my devotion, my commitment. He'd treated it all like a prize he was entitled to claim, leaving me with empty hands, an empty bed, and an even emptier heart.

I thought about the numbers on my app again, remembering the moment I gave up on romance and how I felt when I recognized the absurdity of it all.

Simon and I had built a suite of network security software together. We did it on our own time because we loved constructing castles out of code.

We used to challenge each other to hack our way through our own personally designed protections and safeguards. Who would succeed? Who would be the fastest to break through?

The winner chose which movie we'd watch. Where we'd have dinner.

Who'd be on top later that night.

After Simon sold our software to the company we worked for, he received a huge bonus.

I got nothing.

When I was fired for creating a disturbance in the

workplace, and when my cheating ex-boyfriend and his new lover took out a restraining order on me, that was when I knew what I had to do.

Those two cheaters had escaped me, moving halfway around the world on the money Simon made while using my intellectual property. So I focused on all the other cheaters, locally, through Wandering Hearts.

As I drove away from Ernst's neighborhood, I thought about the names I'd selected. One of them came to mind right away. She'd called herself "KT" on the app. Her real name was Kristine Tippett. KT had wavy brown hair and a cute smile. Her dimpled cheeks transfixed me, but her wide-open eyes told me everything I needed to know. She reminded me of a songbird, a little fluttering twit.

And I knew just the thing to clip that songbird's cheating wings.

9

Noah swapped his flimsy paper coffee cup from hand to hand as he entered the Bureau's conference room the next morning. The reproachful gazes of two agents seated across the table surprised him.

His partner, Eve Taggart, had filled him in on the junior additions. Both had graduated in the top ten percent of their Quantico classes and had chosen Austin as their first assignment. Tall, good-looking, and sporting buzz cuts like their boss had Eve frequently referring to them as the Weston Clones.

Noah avoided their gazes, clenched back a yawn, and pulled out the chair next to Eve. "Thanks for saving me a seat."

She looked down her long nose at him. "Who says that's for you?"

Her sarcastic humor was what he liked most about his partner. While not quite Winter's brand, it was close enough to feel familiar and far better than the icy vibe coming his way from across the table. Noah had yet to meet the other

VCU agents, two of whom had arrived well before him. The other two were away on a field assignment.

You've been here three months and still don't know their names because you haven't spoken with any of them more than a handful of times.

Eve slapped a hand against his shoulder. "You look ready for anything, Dalton. And by that, I mean exhausted. What's up?"

Noah kept his voice low. "Late night. Winter got wrapped up in something with the PD and needed me to pick her up from the station."

"She okay?"

"Fine, yeah. Just wrong place, wrong time. She—"

Noah straightened in his seat when SSA Weston Falkner, a tall man with a head of buzz-cut white hair, stormed into the room. He marched toward the head of the table without acknowledging any of the agents with a look in the eye. His perfectly pressed charcoal suit and navy tie smacked of the precision the supervisory special agent required from his team.

His fierce attention to detail reminded Noah of his best leaders in the Marines. Perhaps because of that, he resented Falkner's tendency to treat him like a mischievous kindergartener.

The SSA dropped his tablet on the table with a *thud*.

He's upset. This is going to be a bitch of a meeting.

"Local PD have asked our assistance regarding two male victims, both dead of stab wounds to the heart. Terry Abbott found at the Black Cat Motel and Ernst Wald found in his home on Cresper Drive."

Noah didn't move a muscle as a spark of worry flared in his belly.

The SSA reached for his tablet and swiped it open, tapping out a quick command that put his screen onto the larger one at the end of the table so he could display two sets of images taken from the crime scenes.

Falkner stepped up to the large screen. "Coroner's report on Wald, the victim on the left, indicates both men may have been killed with the same knife. Wounds are similar, with the same kind of tearing around the entry points."

He returned to the table. "Both men were also found with a gold charm placed on their foreheads…something shaped like a broken heart. I'm still waiting for pictures, but its presence at both scenes means it is likely significant to the killer. I want Cooper and Bevin to look into the jewelry."

Cooper and Bevin. Right. And the other two guys down the hall are called…ah, hell. I'll grab their cards from the front desk. At least I got these guys' names.

Bevin lifted a hand. "Sir, are these the only two cases?"

"So far, yes. But the jewelry and other details have Austin PD worried this could get bigger, fast."

Across the table, the Weston Clones sat up straight, pens in hand ready to take notes.

Falkner's phone chimed. After he checked the device, he swiped his tablet again. The large screen view changed to show gold charms lying on the victims' foreheads, then up close after evidence collection.

"Pictures are in. The charms are heart-shaped, as you can see, with a jagged line etched down the middle. Their significance is yet to be fully proven, but we have reason to believe these men were killed in an act of retribution or revenge for having affairs."

Cooper piped up. "Evidence for that was present at the scene, sir?"

"I'm getting to that, son. Hold your horses."

Falkner focused his attention on his tablet, swiping and scrolling.

Noah felt like anything he said would just earn him more

grief, but he couldn't sit quietly while the clones asked all the questions. "Do we have any more info on the victims, sir? Their lifestyles? Any leads?"

Weston glanced up from the tablet in his hand to meet Noah's eyes but said nothing before turning back to the screen. "Both men had clean records and no history of drugs, gambling, or underworld connections. They were also active on this app."

As he tapped at his tablet, the larger screen showed a dark web site with links to download the Wandering Hearts app.

"Good lord," Eve muttered beside Noah.

"This app is hidden and hidden well. Cyber learned of its relevance when they gained access to the first victim's email accounts. Terry Abbott had traded several messages with users of the app."

Bevin raised a hand. "Sir, has Cyber determined who is behind the app?"

"Not yet. They've located a handful of sites offering download links, and as you can imagine, those sites traffic in the more unsavory, often illicit, aspects of the internet."

Falkner scanned the group as if he expected questions. When nobody offered any, he continued. "We're getting a court order to access the app and acquire the victims' DMs. Wandering Hearts hit the market on March first, just over one week ago. Launch day had somewhere in the neighborhood of a hundred downloads. By the end of the first week, that number was in the thousands and climbing like a rocket to Mars. We'll be over twenty thousand by tomorrow if the trend continues."

"Sir," Agent Cooper butted in, "you mentioned retribution for affairs. I'm assuming Austin PD has already questioned the spouses."

"That's correct. Nellie Abbott was at home with her daughter. She's expressed suspicions about her husband's infidelity. Patricia Wald was away visiting her parents in Dallas and, according to Austin PD, 'had no idea' her husband was seeing another woman."

Noah wanted to ask why Cooper's comment didn't earn him a glare from the SSA, but being petty wouldn't get him anywhere. Swallowing the remark he'd had on his tongue, he focused on the details of the case. "Sir, do we have any indication the killer was a woman? Evidence at the scene or witness statements?"

"No to both questions. Whoever did this, they did it well enough to stay off camera and out of sight. Other than the charms found with both victims, the killer or killers left nothing behind at the scene."

The app roused Noah's curiosity. Killers working dating apps was nothing new, but these two men who used it were murdered within days of this new app's launch.

"How do we know these aren't hits?" Agent Bevin asked. "The wives could've hired someone."

"That'll be something we check into as well. For now, I want you and Cooper canvassing jewelry stores in the area for charms that match what's been found with the victims. If we get any more information from forensics on the charms' origins or supply chain, I'll forward it immediately."

Eve sat forward, hunching over the table. "Sir, I'd like Dalton and I to take interviews with family and friends of the victims."

"You'll be first up on that, Taggart."

The SSA's pointed use of only his partner's name put Noah on edge and had him ready to spit. He held himself steady. "Sir, do I understand correctly that Agent Taggart will be conducting the interviews solo?"

"Yes, you do, Agent Dalton."

"Due respect, sir, I believe I'm an asset on legwork and interviews."

Falkner leveled Noah with a look. "You'll serve this investigation better by helping with the internet searches. You already know how our Cyber team works and are familiar with the logistics of how a killer can hide their ID online. As soon as we get access to the app, you take the lead on that."

Noah cleared his throat, making sure to keep his voice calm. "Backtracking through the dating app could be time-consuming. You said yourself they have nearly twenty thousand users already. If the killer's using a Tor website or a coded VPN, it might be weeks before we find them. If they also use public Wi-Fi networks with Tor, even our top guys could take months to crack it, and that's assuming they can crack it at all."

"And because you're aware of all that, I'm sure you can appreciate why I think you're the best agent for the job."

Falkner closed the tablet's connection with the display screen, his signal that they'd concluded the briefing. But Noah wasn't ready to call it a day, not if doing so meant sitting on his ass in the office with Eve's bamboo plant, Pokey, counting website hits and tracing IP addresses to dead ends.

"Sir, I believe I can do more good in the field."

The SSA slapped his tablet case closed. "Your wife was dragged into the police investigation of the Wald murder. I can't have your involvement raising questions about our objectivity."

Before Noah could challenge his boss, Eve placed her hand over his. "Let it go." She kept her voice to a whisper. "You're not helping yourself."

Noah rocked back in his chair, fuming. Eve had a point, though. Arguing with his boss in front of other agents was a sure way to get his ass busted down to investigating mail fraud.

The SSA departed, followed by Cooper and Bevin. Eve and Noah lagged behind a bit, and when they did leave, he felt like a roped calf straining for freedom.

Eve nudged him with her elbow as they headed to the glorified closet they called their shared office. "You want to tell me what you hope to prove by starting World War III with the SSA?"

Once inside the safety of their own space, he waited to speak until Eve shut the door. "Falkner hates me. He gives me crap jobs and treats me like a damn puppy that's peed on the floor one too many times."

Eve settled into her chair. "Your wife got herself involved in the case. You know damn well Falkner can't let you go out in public on this. He'll get crucified by a D.A. when trying to bring evidence. As far as he's concerned, you're a conflict of interest."

Noah picked up a pen and drummed it against the edge of his desk. "Winter didn't mean to get dragged into a murder investigation."

"But she does do that a lot. And there's only so much looking the other way that anyone around here can do. Even me. Our allegiance has to be to the Bureau. So tread carefully."

Noah knew she was right, but hearing his partner say the words humbled him more than he cared to admit. If push came to shove and Noah made a misstep that shed bad light on the Bureau, he couldn't even count on his partner to back him up.

10

Winter parked her Honda outside the Gardner Grocery distribution building. The unimpressive two-story brick structure was smaller than its neighbors in the city's industrial area, but the fleet of green trucks outside with *Gardner Grocery* in white added a touch of character.

She'd decided to start her investigation into Ernst's murder by talking with Otis Gardner. If, as Ernst claimed, the man had been attempting to intimidate him into dropping his workers' comp claim, he could conceivably have been involved in the man's murder.

If Otis was desperate for cash, he might've freaked out at the prospect of the insurance payments affecting his premiums. But from the look of things, with green delivery trucks moving in and out of the warehouse loading area, Gardner Grocery wasn't in financial trouble.

Maybe Otis Gardner had another reason for wanting Ernst dead.

While Winter knew her intimidation case for Ernst was no longer active, she felt she owed the dead man justice.

Maybe it was the FBI agent in her, but she couldn't just step aside and leave his murder to the authorities.

Not after Darnell "invited" me downtown for no good reason other than getting tired of us crossing paths. News flash, Detective Davenport, I'm here to stay.

The bay where trucks waited to make deliveries to the local stores in town was a hub of activity with people in green coveralls loading produce and goods into the van boxes.

No one noticed when Winter slipped through the loading area and walked inside.

Crates, bins of produce, and endless rows of shelving packed the facility's first floor. More employees in green carried tablets like bees swarming in a hive as they checked the inventory. The operation impressed Winter. Gardner had at least fifty employees managing his distribution center.

She strolled the aisles between metal shelves, devising a plan for how to sell her sudden appearance to Otis Gardner. She hoped he'd be reasonable. It'd make getting what she needed much easier—whether that was proof that he'd been intimidating Ernst Wald or that he'd somehow been involved in the man's death.

She rounded a rack of shelves and found a glassed-in office space. She was almost to the door when a chubby man in a too-small suit walked out.

"Winter Black, is it? The police were just here about Ernst's murder and your name was mentioned several times. I suspected you would show up but thought you would be decent enough to use the front door. I'm Otis Gardner, by the way, founder and owner of the company on whose grounds you are currently trespassing."

Winter should've realized the police would check up on her story. She wished she'd called ahead of her arrival, but

her lack of sleep and fixation on finding the killer had left
her off her game.

She tucked a loose lock of hair back into her ponytail.
"Yes, I was taken in for questioning because I arrived at
Ernst's house shortly after he'd been found. I was there to
rule out the possibility that his insurance claim was
fraudulent, before expending any more time on his case."

"It seems a murderer has made that a moot point, and I
still don't understand why you're here." Gardner's eyebrows
shot up, as if demanding the explanation Winter had yet to
provide.

But she wasn't ready to play ball with the brusque man.
"Do you have any idea who killed him?"

"No. Just as I told the police. Now your purpose, please,
or I'll be calling them back to remove you."

Winter noted the slight uptick of anger in his voice. "I'm
not here to upset anyone. I just wanted to know more about
Ernst."

Gardner rubbed his hand across his chin. "You're not a
cop, just a P.I. who works insurance fraud and divorce cases.
What are you hoping to learn by harassing my employees?"

The cutting remark had Winter digging her nails into the
palm of her hand. "Ernst Wald was my client, and regardless
of any fraud he may or may not have engaged in…with
regard to his insurance claim…I feel I owe it to him to help
the police in any way I can. My interest in a case doesn't end
when the subject of my investigation dies, just like your
concern about a former employee didn't end when he left
your employ."

Winter waited for the man to spit fire, but he remained
cool and never darted his gaze from hers. He stiffened where
he stood, then stepped to the side and held out a hand,
gesturing for her to precede him into the all-glass office
space.

"A few of my staff would be happy to talk to you about Ernst. My secretary, Betty Anne, knew him best. You might want to start with her." He opened the glass door for her. "Shall we?"

Winter couldn't help but inwardly groan as she walked through.

Whatever you and Wald were doing on that app, it rattled you enough to play damage control. I'm guessing Betty Anne will be a fountain of worthless information.

The ringing phones and tapping keyboards were a stark contrast to the din of the forklifts and shouting on the warehouse floor.

Gardner guided her to the right and stopped before the desk of a middle-aged woman with gray-tinged hair and deep-red lipstick. She stared over her wire-rimmed glasses at Winter, sizing her up with bold brown eyes.

"Betty Anne, this is Winter Black. She wants to ask you a few questions about Ernst." Otis glanced at Winter. "She's a private investigator hired to look into his death."

Winter caught the hint. It seemed the owner of Gardner Grocery didn't want his staff to discover what had really inspired Winter's visit.

Damage Control 101. Own the narrative.

Betty put down the pen in her hand and offered a sad smile. "Mr. Wald was a kind man. I was very sorry to hear of his passing."

Passing? She made his fatal stab wound sound so peaceful, like he died in his sleep.

Otis Gardner tapped the edge of the desk with his chubby finger. "Get Ms. Black anything she might need. And I'll need that first quarterly from Tom before the day is out."

She had to commend Gardner. He could be slick when he needed to be.

The man waddled away, putting on a hearty smile for his

staff and pausing at a few other people's desks to trade brief remarks or chitchat. The moment he slipped behind a half-open door to the back of the office, Winter noticed how Betty Anne's grin vanished.

She folded her hands atop her desk. "Let's get one thing straight, Ms. Black. I'm not a fool, and secrets have a way of becoming facts inside this office."

To call the woman rattled would be an understatement. Winter waited until Betty Anne composed herself. "Are there any secrets you'd be comfortable sharing with me?"

"You want to know what the police wanted. Where did Ernst go after work? Who did he see behind his wife's back?"

Winter cocked her head. "They asked you that?"

She nodded. "I wasn't blind. Patricia adored him, but he treated her like dirt. He was always hunting for action online. The cheating bastard. Probably the same as that Abbott person from the news, the one they found murdered at the Black Cat."

Had the police released the first victim's name already? Winter hadn't checked the news yet that morning.

With wariness tickling the back of her neck, Winter inched closer. "Which desk was Ernst's when he worked here?"

Betty Anne pointed at one just to the right of hers that faced the glass wall and overlooked the warehouse floor.

She could see his computer screen easily. Unless he sat really close or turned it to the side for privacy.

"Any chance you know which sites he used? Maybe he told you about them, or…"

Betty Anne offered her a venomous smile. "Yes, I could see what he was doing. That's how I know he was scrolling dating profiles instead of working."

Winter kept her gaze on the desk where Ernst had once

sat. "Would you know how I could get in touch with his wife?"

"I'll get you her phone number."

She took her time jotting down Patricia Wald's name and two phone numbers. Winter examined Betty Anne's hands, searching for any signs of defensive wounds or other indications that the woman had recently engaged in an act of extreme violence.

No dark marks under her fingernails or around the cuticle. She'd have washed the blood off and scrubbed well, but sometimes a killer misses a tiny dot.

"Ms. Black?"

Winter startled as Betty Anne rotated her chair, forcing Winter back a step. "Yes?"

The woman held up the sticky note with Patricia Wald's name and number. "Between you and me, I think Otis was right about Ernst, just for the wrong reasons."

Winter schooled her face to appear curious. "What do you mean?"

"His insurance claim was legit, and Otis knew it. But Otis panics about anything to do with money. I'd bet he has something he wanted to keep hidden and couldn't trust Ernst not to blab about. My guess would be it's something to do with all those dating apps Ernst was always on."

Winter stood up straight, glancing around the office. The other employees all had their heads down over their work, some wearing headphones or earbuds.

"Does Otis use any monitoring software in the office?"

The secretary studied her before turning back to her computer. "No, thank goodness. I could never work in a place that watches every move I make. Otis isn't the nicest man in the world, but he at least understands and values autonomy."

"What about Ernst's autonomous use of company resources to set up dates? Ever mention that to the boss?"

Betty Anne's laugh sounded like shattering crystal. "Oh, no. At least, not in so many words. I told him he might want to ensure Ernst's use of company computers was in line with regulations. He got my meaning, but that was probably because he was guilty of the same thing."

"You saw Otis Gardner on dating sites too?"

The woman gave a confident nod. "I've known Otis for twenty years. Ever since I started working for the man, he's been straying. His wife doesn't deserve that kind of treatment. No woman does. But I couldn't very well tell him that to his face, now, could I?"

"So why rat on Ernst? Why not just tell him directly? If you've worked here twenty years, you have to have some rapport with the man. Don't you?"

Betty Anne rolled her eyes. "Ms. Black, when you have several years of spare time, I'll tell you all the ways you don't make an impression on Otis Gardner. He's an ox, or a pig, depending on who you ask. Either way, you won't change his course with a few well-intentioned words."

That put Winter's mind back on the conversation Wald claimed to have had with Gardner about the app, and how things with his workers' comp went south after that. Betty's explanation sounded innocuous enough, but could Winter's dead client have tried to coerce his boss somehow, perhaps with a threat to reveal his online activity?

"Ernst mentioned an intimidating email from Otis. Any idea what it was about?"

The secretary laughed out loud again, briefly stirring a few other employees from their work. "Intimidating? Oh dear, no. I keep Otis's calendar and read all his business emails. He hasn't sent anything to Ernst since the man's injury."

"What about a private email address?"

Betty Anne huffed. "I suppose, but that doesn't sound like Otis to me. He's a scoundrel and will lie to your face if he thinks it'll net him anything. And he knows he's a cheat. But private emails? Burner phones? He's not that…sophisticated."

That was a damning estimation of the man if Winter had ever heard one.

Winter noted the nameplate on Betty Anne's desk, which showed her full name, hyphenated as Rose-Thomas. Resolving to look into the woman's history later, she changed tracks, hoping to get more about Wald's online activities. If she could find out which sites he used, maybe that could get her the link she needed to help solve his murder.

"Betty Anne, when Ernst hired me, he mentioned an app he and Otis both used. He didn't give me a name. I know it's a long shot, but do you know anything about that?"

With a knowing smile on her lips, the secretary clicked over to a window view displaying her own email inbox. She scrolled down to a folder marked *Otis archived*. A few more clicks had her bringing up an email sent from a personal account.

"I'm guessing you mean this? Otis didn't respond and deleted it, but I kept a copy, just in case. You never know when you're going to need dirt on the boss, right?"

"So Otis didn't send Ernst any emails, but Ernst sent Otis one?"

"Yes, ma'am. Well, it doesn't have Ernst's full name on it, per se, but it's him."

Winter's eyes rounded in disgust as she read the email Betty Anne pulled up.

"I'll spare you the picture he attached. Nothing every woman on Earth hasn't seen before."

"Can you forward that email to me?" Winter slid her

business card onto Betty Anne's desk. She read the message from Wald's personal email again as the woman sent it to her work address.

Hey Boss,

Check out this tasty treat I just found on WH. Gonna try for next Monday. Good luck on your search. LOL

E

"What's 'WH?'"

"It's got to be one of those dating profiles he and Otis were using."

As if he'd been listening somehow, Otis himself called to Betty Anne from across the office area. "When Ms. Black is done consuming your limited time, I'd like a review of last week's numbers for our corporate clients, please."

Winter winked at Betty Anne. "Guess that's my cue."

"I suppose so, and I hope I've been helpful." She lowered her voice. "If it makes any difference, I'm retiring next Tuesday. Otis doesn't know yet, and you can bet that's something I'm going to enjoy telling him directly, right before I walk out the door."

Offering a thank-you, Winter made a quick exit from the office and the facility. As she got in her vehicle, she mulled over what she learned from Betty Anne.

That email could end up as material evidence. I'll have to tell Darnell about it if Gardner's implicated.

If both Wald and Gardner were active on dating profiles, that might relate to motive. Aside from Wald's sleazy and juvenile email, sent after his fight with Gardner about workers' comp, Winter had no reason to believe Wald was blackmailing his boss.

If anything, Betty Anne Rose-Thomas was the one better positioned to blackmail her employer.

Why would she want to do that? Unless she has history with him outside of being a long-term employee.

Thinking about Wald again, Winter considered the idea that he might have threatened to tell Gardner's wife about the dating app. But if he had, Gardner could've done the same thing. Both men would suffer in their own well-deserved way.

None of that spells out murder.

Dating app killers were nothing new, and if that were the case here, Winter knew she'd be sidelined the instant Darnell put the pieces together. If she were going to learn anything that might help the police—and get her back into Darnell's good books—this was her chance.

She pulled out of the Gardner Grocery parking lot with Patricia Wald's number running through her mind. Winter had new information about the woman's husband. Now she needed anything that might help her discover a connection between him and Terry Abbott, beyond the dating app they both used. Why did one killer target these two men?

What had Noah said during the Electrocutioner case?

"I guess it's time to go *cherchez la femme.*"

11

Ona's Coffee Shop smelled of cinnamon and sugar even more than freshly brewed coffee. Winter sat at a wobbly wooden table by the door with a mocha warming her hands while she kept watch for Patricia Wald. She was supposed to arrive around two thirty but had said she might be a bit late.

Winter spent the time scouring the internet for any dating apps with the initials WH. She almost gave up until she spotted a forum post with a link to a dark web site to download Wandering Hearts.

Unlike just about every other dating app Winter had heard of, this one specifically advertised to "those locked in holy matrimony but still feeling a need to run free."

Well, there's an ad campaign. This app's not sparing any punches.

With that question answered, Winter made a mental note to dig into the app once she returned to her office before stalking Patricia's late husband's social media. She found a picture of the couple, which would hopefully help her spot the slender brunette when she walked in.

With any luck, the widow would be as forthcoming with details about her husband as Betty Anne had been.

The tinkle of the bell above the door drew Winter's gaze to the entrance. A demure, fragile woman wearing an ill-fitting, dark-blue running suit stepped inside. She peered around the shop, clutching at the purse strap slung over her right shoulder.

Winter stood to attract her attention.

The widow's beauty blossomed behind a slight grin. "Ms. Black?" She approached Winter's table. "I was surprised to hear from you."

Winter motioned to a seat across from hers. "Thank you for coming, Mrs. Wald. Can I get you a coffee or a—"

"Nothing." She waved a tapered hand. "Thank you. And call me Patricia. My stomach can't take anything right now. The past twenty-four hours have been…" She let the sentence hang as she sank into her chair.

It hadn't even been that long since her husband's murder, but grief and lack of sleep had a way of warping time. Winter pushed her coffee cup aside. "I want to offer my deepest condolences. I know there's nothing I can say to make this easier, but I want to assure you I'm here to help."

Patricia set her purse on the table. "I'm not sure how you can. The police already questioned me. They told me what happened. Every horrible detail. I'm supposed to meet with someone from the FBI tomorrow morning."

When she sniffled, Winter offered her a napkin from the dispenser on the table. "I can imagine how rough that must've been."

Dabbing at her eyes, Patricia held in a sob. "I'm not sure I can ever go back to my house. I slept at my sister's last night. I work from home running a temp agency, and I can't even do that. And with Ernst gone, I need the money more than ever, but he…"

Winter tried to find a gentle way to ask what was at the forefront of her mind. It seemed clear enough that Patricia Wald knew of her husband's infidelity, now that the police had told her, but her demeanor could just as well be due to simple grief.

"How much did the police tell you about," she placed her hand on the table, tensing, "who might've murdered Ernst?"

"I don't know anyone who'd want my husband dead." Patricia crumpled the napkin in her hand, and her face went stony. "But I'd kill him myself if he were still alive."

"You didn't say that during the interview, did you? To the cops?"

She shook her head. Her returning sadness pulled her mouth into a frown as her eyes welled with tears. "No. I never suspected Ernst was unhappy. I'd have left him in an instant if I knew he was looking to meet other women."

Winter pressed into the table. "I talked to Betty Anne at Gardner Grocery."

"She's nice. She's a good person. I just wish she'd told me Ernst was cheating. I could've divorced him before all this happened, and then I wouldn't have to…" Stifling a sob with the crumpled napkin, Patricia turned away, her shoulders shaking."

"I'm so sorry." Winter's heart broke for the woman.

After a few deep breaths, Patricia composed herself and faced Winter again. "Why were you talking to Betty Anne?"

Winter scanned the nearby tables. "I went there to follow up on Ernst's behalf. He'd hired me to prove Otis Gardner was intimidating him into dropping his disability claim and—"

"Ernst was legitimately injured."

Winter sat back in her seat. "I never said he wasn't. When I spoke to Betty Anne, she told me Ernst was active online. She handles a lot of Otis Gardner's email and spotted a message between them referencing an app called Wandering Hearts. Gardner was active online too."

With a sniff of disgust, Patricia grabbed Winter's coffee and took a swallow, apologizing for not asking first as she set the cup down.

"It's fine. You can finish it if you'd like."

The woman offered a weak laugh and wiped at her eyes again. "For a minute there, I hoped it had whiskey in it."

"Sorry, still not five o'clock, and I'm the only one driving me anywhere."

"Of course." She paused to take another sip of the coffee. "You were saying Otis was a cheater too. This is my surprised face." Across the table, a blank-faced Patricia Wald wadded up her napkin and snagged another to blow her nose. "I should've known he was unhappy. Bored, whatever. Seen the signs, you know?"

Winter reached across the table for her hand. "This has nothing to do with you. It was his mistake not to cherish what he had at home. Don't you ever feel guilty for his choices." She sat back, meeting the other woman's tear-reddened eyes. "Patricia, this might sound odd, but can you tell me if you've ever heard of a Terry Abbott?"

"You mean the guy they found at the Cat? Not until I saw the news this morning. The police department had a press briefing about Ernst and mentioned somebody named Abbott when they asked people to call in with information."

That answered Winter's question about how Betty Anne might have learned Terry Abbott's name.

"Patricia, I want you to call me if you think of anything, no matter how slight. It could be important."

While Winter rifled through her messenger bag for a business card, Patricia released a long sigh.

"You sound like that detective who questioned me. Davenport."

She handed Patricia her card. "Davenport's a good cop."

Winter knew she owed the man some credit for helping her in the past. Even if he had turned her stakeout gone wrong into an "interrogation" in the interview room downtown.

Maybe you're in my pocket now, Darnell. Or maybe we'll be even once I fill you in on the Wandering Hearts app.

Patricia tucked the business card away in her purse and stood. "Thank you, Ms. Black—"

"Winter, please. No need to be formal."

The widow sniffed, and the beginnings of a smile curled her mouth before a fierce sob overtook her. Winter pushed another few napkins her way and waited while she composed herself.

Patricia Wald finally exited the coffee shop, but on shaky legs.

However angry the widow might've been at her husband's infidelity, that feeling couldn't erase the sorrow of losing him so suddenly and violently.

Processing their conversation, Winter found no reason to consider Patricia guilty of the crime. Either she was an exceptional actor, or the woman was grief-stricken and doing her best to stay afloat.

She decided to share what she'd learned with Darnell, calling him as she drove back to her office. At the very least, she might mend the bridges enough to earn herself some help with the next client to grace her door.

He picked up after four rings. To her surprise, he was neither impressed nor dismissive with what she had to share.

"Some dating app called Wandering Hearts connects Ernst Wald and his employer? Thank you for that, Ms. Black. We'll look into it."

"Otis Gardner might be at risk as well. If the killer's using the app to track victims…"

"Yes, I understand that's a possibility. We'll look into it and maybe have patrol check in on the grocery man. Just in case. Thank you again."

He ended the call, leaving Winter to wonder how much new information she'd really provided. It sure sounded as if Darnell knew about the app already.

So I'm back at square one. Clientless, and with no real prospects on the horizon beyond delivering summons for understaffed law offices.

Now if I could just stop thinking about solving this murder mystery for five seconds...

Winter knew the likelihood of that ever happening. She might not wear a badge or carry federal identification anymore, but she was still just as devoted to stopping killers as she'd ever been. Especially when the victims were her clients.

12

Back at her office, Winter downloaded and opened a browser with Tor connectivity to dig into the Wandering Hearts app. Thankfully, both Kline and Ariel had left for the day, so she didn't have to worry about them peering over her shoulder.

Ariel's taste for investigative work bordered on nosiness sometimes. Kline remained fixed in his concern for Winter's well-being, so much so that she could almost feel him scolding her for even perusing a dating app.

She scrolled through her first search results, which only included forum comments about how awesome Wandering Hearts could be. As her finger worked the mouse wheel, Kline's gruff voice filled her mind.

What're you lookin' at that stuff for? Don't tell me you and that man of yours are splitting up.

Pushing those accusatory thoughts aside, Winter ran a new search, adjusting her terms to focus on obtaining the app via download.

Bingo!

Multiple forums offered links that directed potential

users to a plain page with a background styled like a brown paper bag. The top and bottom corners of the bag were all folded back, revealing a hint of a woman's thigh, a man's muscular shoulder, and various tongues curled over parted lips.

A ticker ran across the top of the download page. *Nobody will ever know unless you tell them. Your digital trail can't be traced.*

The Wandering Hearts app promised users a "digitally risk-free" hookup experience.

Winter knew digital forensic work could uncover connections and online activity that people would swear they'd kept hidden. But the dark web was also a reality that hosted sites the FBI still had trouble penetrating.

Wandering Hearts had to be making promises its designers knew they couldn't keep with the hope of attracting users. If their membership counter was anything to go by, their tactics were working.

She pulled out her tablet, thinking it was safer to explore the app there rather than on her phone. It was an older iPad she'd been meaning to replace someday soon.

If this app loads it up with malware, that day may be tomorrow.

Once she'd navigated to the download link and installed the app on her tablet, she spent an hour sifting through user profiles. The app only included residents of Austin and nearby suburbs.

Still, the number of potential adulterers in the Austin area alone could keep divorce attorneys gainfully employed for decades, assuming the injured spouse wasn't on the app too.

She decided to study who used the app. How many men versus how many women?

The app didn't propose to exclude any orientations and

offered multiple options, including a "decline to state" choice under "gender."

If Terry Abbott and Ernst Wald had been stalked on the app and killed by the same person, and assuming both men were truly heterosexual, the killer could be female. Both Ernst Wald and Terry Abbott's public-facing profile pages were marked as "man seeking woman." That could make male users identifying as heterosexual likelier targets.

But two murders aren't necessarily a pattern. The charm calling card is, though.

Running a custom search for users identifying as male returned a significant majority of profiles. Of the nearly twenty thousand users, close to eighty-five percent were men. Winter had no way of knowing how many of these men paid to use the app, which would grant them more privacy options and access to the app's internal messaging service.

After ninety minutes, she was still no closer to understanding how Wald's use of the app was connected to his murder or if the killer had simply grabbed his name at random. Or had the killer been watching their victims? Maybe the perpetrator had been stalking their prey.

The thought of being watched forced Winter to stand from her desk and pace the small confines of her office. Feeling exposed, she examined the room and decided to do a quick sweep for hidden cameras, on the chance that Kline had missed something.

You're being paranoid.

But she searched anyway.

After scouring every corner and the underside of every desk and shelf, she gave up. The office was surveillance free. Her phone pinged with a text from Ariel as she gathered her messenger bag and headed for the door.

I'm at Magro's Villa with Tom tonight. 7PM. Wish me luck!

Ariel had left early for another date, with a promise to

text Winter where she'd be going and the time of her dinner reservation. She'd also call as soon as she got home.

Winter was proud of her assistant for taking those precautions. Ariel had her head on straight enough to think of her safety first.

Finding a boyfriend hadn't been high on her list of priorities when Winter hired her, but she'd been making more noises about it recently.

Winter sent her a quick *Have fun* text back and warned her to stay off Wandering Hearts, just in case.

Ariel fired back a reply right away. *Whaaat is Wandering Hearts and why does my married boss know about it?*

Rolling her eyes, Winter shot another message back. *Your married P.I. boss is working a case. Details later. Have a good date :P*

Tossing her phone into her messenger bag, Winter headed home.

All these thoughts of other people getting romantic has me missing a certain Texan I would never dream of wandering away from.

When she got home, Noah was still at work. She'd texted before leaving her office, but he hadn't replied yet.

She stepped into the kitchen and opened a bottle of his favorite wine. She'd let it breathe a bit while she figured out what kind of food would pair well with the red blend, so she'd know what to order in.

Opening her phone, she looked for a wine review site. Her search returned a list of hits that included every dating app she'd ever heard of, including a few new ones she wished she hadn't.

Damn algorithm has my number, I guess.

With curiosity eating at her, Winter opened her tablet again to explore the Wandering Hearts app.

When the front door opened, she slapped her tablet face down on the counter.

"I'm home," Noah sang.

A moment later, he came in from the front room, holding his face in his hands. Once he dropped his hands, Winter saw the fatigue in his eyes.

"Tough day? I wish I could say I made dinner, but the best I managed was to open a bottle of wine. I can make reservations, though. What sounds good?"

He laughed before pulling her in to a hug, his arms circling her waist. "You sound good. Just you."

She leaned forward, collapsing into his warm scent. He relaxed his embrace and stood back, not meeting her eyes.

"What happened at work?"

Noah continued to examine the walls instead of her. "Falkner has me running in place while the rest of the team is on field work. I feel like I've been benched, and it's because…"

"Because?"

He finally settled his gaze onto hers. "The whole team knows you were pulled in by Austin PD, so I'm on restricted duty for this case."

Winter flipped her tablet face up. "Does it have anything to do with this app?"

His eyes went wide, and he flashed her a warning look. "What the hell're you doing on there?"

"So I was right. What does the Bureau know about it? Two men are dead, one of them a client, and they were both using it." She stepped closer to him, putting a hand on his chest. "So, Agent Dalton, how about you read me in on all the dirty details?"

A smile lit up his face, and he placed a hand over hers. "I wish I could, but how about we figure out dinner first? We can have all the dirty talk you want after."

She wrinkled her nose and pressed against his chest, guiding him back into the front room and walking him up against the arm of the couch. With a gentle shove, she pushed him onto his back and climbed over the couch arm to join him.

13

After working up an appetite with Winter, Noah didn't exactly have the energy to whip up dinner for them both, but he did it anyway. None of their favorite takeout places sounded appealing, and he couldn't trust Winter's cooking. He smiled at her as he bit into his sautéed brook trout and she sipped her wine.

"You know," Winter teased as she leaned back against the kitchen counter opposite him, "we could make this a regular thing."

"What's that? Me cooking dinner, or…"

"Or?"

They laughed together, and Noah's shoulders relaxed, the weight of his day fading from his mind. Winter, however, was ready to remind him of it all over again.

"You mentioned some missing information that would help me with my case. Care to put those cards on the table?"

He swallowed and took a sip from his glass. "That reminds me," he gestured around them with his fork, "we still need to get a dining table."

"Nice dodge, Dalton. But I wasn't asking about furniture. This case—"

"Winter, this case—"

"—involved my client, my business."

He set his plate on the counter behind him and turned back to her. "Falkner's got me digging into that app and its users, trying to find leads to the killer. You and I both know how long it's going to take to get anywhere on that."

She nodded. "And more bodies could hit the ground before then."

"Exactly. Falkner has his clones working another angle, which has to be our best shot. That's the piece you're missing."

"Okay, so help me un-miss it. And tell me about these clones. They sound fun."

Noah allowed himself another laugh before retrieving his plate and taking another bite of his dinner. "Cooper and Bevin. The walking, talking, dressing-just-like Falkner guys. Eve calls them the Weston Clones."

"And the info?"

He told her about the heart charms found on both bodies. "They've got to be easy to track down. Heck, I could probably find the charms online with a quick search, and I'm sure the clones have already done that."

She cleaned off the last bit of fish from her plate and sipped more of her wine. "If so, then they're benched, too, right? Unless they found a retailer in the area."

"Maybe. Or they're joining Eve. She's handling interviews with affected family and the Black Cat's manager."

Winter recounted how she'd spoken with Patricia Wald earlier and managed only to confirm that both Terry Abbott and Ernst Wald had been on the Wandering Hearts app. "I brought it up to Darnell that I knew of three men who were active on it."

"Two of those men are already dead. Who's the other one?"

"Otis Gardner, the man I was supposed to be investigating for a harassment case for Ernst Wald."

"What'd Darnell have to say about all that?"

"He basically blew it off. Gave me the line about 'looking into it' and thanked me for my service."

"Welcome to the veterans club."

She gently kicked him in the shin. "Smart-ass."

"Nope, just a Marine. But back to the idea of this being 'your case.' We need to be careful. Somebody's using that app to hunt for victims. They're really good at covering their tracks."

"That's true. But you were right that we have to consider other options. I spoke to Otis's secretary, Betty Anne. She had plenty of opportunity to monitor both Ernst Wald's and Otis Gardner's online activities. She showed me an email from Wald to Gardner without any hesitation."

"You think she could be involved somehow?"

"I don't know. A knife is a personal weapon, one that takes conviction to employ, and that indicates the killer likely knew the victims. Betty Anne didn't strike me as the killing type at first. Now that I'm thinking about that app, though…she had strong opinions about her boss and coworker being cheaters. Infidelity doesn't sit well with that woman."

Noah swirled his wine before using it to wash down the last bite of his dinner. "Could be a person of interest, at least. I'd mention her to Falkner, but he'd just holler at me for discussing the case with you. What about dropping an anonymous tip with Darnell?"

"I could do that, but I hate the thought of making trouble for Betty Anne if she's not the murderer. She's set to retire next Tuesday and was looking forward to telling Otis as she was walking out the door. It sounded like she wants to stick it to him, figuratively."

"What if she intends to make it literal as well?"

Winter shook her head, her shiny black hair swaying around her shoulders. "Killing him right as she leaves his employ doesn't make sense. As an employee who had years to build up resentment, which she made no effort to hide when we spoke, she'd be an obvious suspect."

"And she knows him and one of the two victims. Any chance she knew Terry Abbott?"

"I don't think so. She called him 'that Abbott person from the news.'"

He leaned back and considered their damnably few options. He was hamstrung by his career and obligation to procedure, and she was effectively working off the clock, even if one of the murder victims had been her client. "Here's a crazy idea. What if we set up a fake profile? Falkner'll probably have me do that, anyway, but if we have our own, we can access the information as we choose."

"That *is* a crazy idea. I'm kinda shocked you didn't let me come up with it first. Who are you and what have you done with my husband the FBI agent?"

He chuckled, but conceded her point with a finger by making a tick mark in the air.

"One in your column. But I still think it's the way to go with this case. If we're both working that angle, it'll go faster. Otherwise, I'll be stuck sifting through user profiles until the damn cows come home."

It would be a risk, both personally and professionally. If anyone they knew spotted the profiles, they could lose friends due to the wrong assumptions. Noah could lose his job. Winter also stood to lose her reputation if the news got out about her using an app designed to enable infidelity—no matter how she tried to spin it.

Before Winter could say anything, Noah put up his hand. "You know what, this is a dumb idea. Forget I mentioned it."

"No. It's crazy and probably dumb, sure, but we could dig into the case."

"What if someone we know is on there? What if the Weston Clones spot us?"

"So we don't use photos. It'll probably reduce the number of hits we get, but plenty of people are on dating apps and sites anonymously, or use AI-generated photos. At least, until they get a connection going around shared interests or values."

She was right, and the familiar burn of tension burned in Noah's gut. Working this case so far had been nothing but tedium and promised to be more of the same if he didn't take action on his own.

"I'll still have to stay out of the mix. If Falkner gets the slightest hint I'm pursuing this outside of his purview, I'm toast."

"We can manage it without implicating you at all. I'll ask Ariel to help too. She's been spending time with a guy lately and probably knows all the lingo of the contemporary dating scene."

"Fair enough, but tell her to be careful. No photos, and nothing that could tie her back to you or your business."

With a nod, Winter cleared their plates from the counter and started filling the sink. "I'll look into the jewelry too. You'll probably get details from the Falkner Twins, but it can't hurt to have another set of eyes on the task."

"Especially when those eyes are so lovely." He reached up and drew her mouth down to his for a kiss. After they parted, she fished out the dishwashing gloves from under the sink. Noah stood back as she added soap to the water. "They're the Weston Clones, by the way. Not twins. You gotta get it right, or Eve'll put you in a time-out in the corner with Pokey."

Groaning, she slapped the rubber gloves onto the counter beside him. "You're on cleanup detail for that one, Dalton. I'm going to shower."

Noah set to work. In moments like this, when their easy banter and playful sparring warmed his heart, he could almost forget about the constant threat of danger outside.

14

The annoying electronic music pounding in the bar wasn't my thing. I'd had enough thumping and pumping bass to last a lifetime. Simon had always insisted on playing drum and bass music when we had sex, because he was afraid people in the neighboring apartments might hear us.

Like the sounds of lovemaking were offensive or the act itself a crime to keep hidden.

I preferred romantic ballads...tunes about lovers finding happiness in the end. My second girlfriend once compared my music taste to that of a thirteen-year-old girl. That night, I took sweet revenge by dropping a roofie into her drink. It wasn't my fault she ended up in the hospital and nearly died.

The music in the bar shifted to a rap song. The beat remained heavy and matched the lyrics, which were all about sexual conquest and the rapper's prowess. As if he were a gift from God, delivering the poor masses from a pleasureless existence.

He sounds like the perfect sort of person to remove from circulation. That attitude is exactly why so many people cheat in the first place.

They'd been trained to believe wild nights of sexual thrill were evidence of true love. No wonder people fled their commitments. They were too fixated on finding the ultimate sexual experience and dismissed anything short of mind-blowing.

I knew what I liked and what I wanted in a partner. And I knew it didn't exist. Not in this world of cheaters, liars, and romance thieves. People who'd take what they could get and rush off to the next bed down the road.

For them, love was a commodity. The more notches on their bedpost, the better they felt about themselves. At least until the glow wore off and the dull monotony of life threatened to consume them.

They feel that way because they're blind to what real love looks like. Real love is day-to-day. It's not sitting in a shitty bar listening to music that bumps and grinds against your eardrums.

But I had to sit here and wait for KT to show up. She'd insisted on this bar because her wife "would never go to a place like that," so the chances of us being seen together were nil.

As much as I hated supporting a cheater's way of thinking, I had to admit her choice worked in my favor.

KT's internet footprint and social media accounts were full of loving pictures of her with her wife and their pet dog, Merlot, showcasing a seemingly happy life. But KT was unfaithful. Why else would she be on my app?

And she said her wife was "boring" and their relationship had "grown stale."

I almost spit up my drink thinking about how easily KT had thrown aside her commitment, simply because the relationship no longer felt new and exciting.

Whose fault is that? I wanted to ask. I already knew the answer. KT's wife wasn't on the app. She was too busy managing her home decor business and taking Merlot for walks while KT tried to build a following on her YouTube channel as an amateur musician.

Killing KT would remove one more cheater from the world and save her wife the heartache of realizing their marriage was doomed from the start.

I understood all too well what those forgotten by their unfaithful partners endured.

Searching the powdered, painted, and Botoxed faces at the bar, I almost fled the room. The palpable desperation on display had me ready to vomit. The headache-inducing music added to my misery as I hunted for Kristine Tippett.

She'd begged for this meeting, wanting to assure herself I was normal. I almost took her off my list, thinking that perhaps she was simply curious and didn't mean to go through with any actual infidelity. But she'd also chosen the venue, and that gave me a glimpse into her reckless character.

Anyone looking for a meaningless roll in the sheets would choose a noisy, public spot to talk and exchange ideas. Call me old-fashioned, but nothing good ever developed in a bar with fancy umbrella drinks and the faint aroma of bleach.

I stood up from the barstool and passed a few couples deep in conversation. Beneath the swirling lights and pounding speakers hanging from the ceiling, I made a circuit around the dance floor.

My path took me around couples reflecting every sexual preference and identity under the sun.

Near the end of the bar, I spotted a woman sitting alone sipping a wine spritzer.

I bet this is my girl.

I dug out my phone, and despite a few nudges from patrons crowding past me, found the woman pictured on my app to be the same spritzer-sipping woman.

Well, hello, Kristine.

My prey eagerly scanned the establishment with her pretty brown eyes. She appeared worried I wouldn't show. I smiled. I had big plans for her.

I'd teach her the lesson she desperately needed to learn and save her wife years of heartache in the process. All the nights spent wondering when Kristine would come home. Where she was and who she was with. All the tears cried, knowing she was cheating.

How long before she snapped and killed Kristine herself?

I was doing the world a service and saving people from ending up like me. Imagine a world overflowing with coldhearted killers.

My smile transformed into a grin when I sat next to Kristine. Her eyes widened, and I could tell she liked what she saw.

She nervously played with the straw in her drink. "Alex? That's the name you gave me in the chat. I don't need to know your real name." Her laugh reminded me of hard candies being dumped into a dish. Kristine was all sweetness and bright colors, but I recognized the snake hiding inside her skin.

I twirled a lock of her hair around my finger. "If Alex is who you want me to be, then that's who I am tonight, KT."

She stared at the black gloves on my hands. "What are those for?"

"My hands get cold easily. It's a medical condition. Nothing with scars or rashes, just a circulation issue."

Kristine checked the bar around them. "I've never done this before. I love my wife still, really. But you know how it goes. After the honeymoon wears off…things become boring in the bedroom. I need more."

"I understand."

She sipped her drink. "Your profile pics make me think

you're the right woman for the job, but I haven't seen anything to prove I'm talking to the same person I met on the app. Care to go someplace where you can reveal the evidence?"

I wanted to take her then and there, to reach into my bag and pull the blade I'd claimed from Terry as the tool of my new profession. I wanted to sink my weapon into Kristine's chest, pushing down with both hands to pierce her cheating heart.

But that would have to wait. This wasn't the right place for such an act. Our next date would be our last, and I couldn't wait to make all of Kristine's fantasies come true.

"Let's stretch out the anticipation, shall we? How about Thursday night for a truly revealing performance?"

"That sounds great. I can't wait."

Oh, I bet you can't, Kristine. If only you knew what you were waiting for.

15

A nippy morning breeze tossed around trash on the street as Winter shuffled inside her office, balancing her messenger bag against her hip while holding a mocha. She got in just as Ariel was popping up from her desk.

"Sorry about that. I would've let you in, but…"

Her assistant's usual bubbly demeanor had clearly deflated at some point since they last spoke.

"How'd last night go? From the look on your face, I'm guessing it was a bust."

Ariel sighed and rounded her desk, dropping into her chair as Winter set down her messenger bag. She pulled up one of the chairs set aside for waiting clients and placed her mocha on Ariel's desk.

"He was a dick. Dinner, dancing, drinks. All of that was great. When I suggested separate Ubers, he got all spiky and called me a tease. I don't know this guy from Adam. We've had two dates, and he expects me to go home with him?"

"Sorry to hear that, but dating in the new millennium doesn't sound much different from dating in the old one."

"Weren't you, like, five in 1999?"

"Sure, something like that, and we'll leave that unconfirmed for now. My point still stands. Dating isn't easy, and sometimes people are only out for a hookup. You have to know that, right?"

Ariel scoffed. "Yes, I do, but you'd think honesty might...I don't know, cross people's minds. It's not like I found this guy on a hookup app. He was on Lifetime Lovelines for crying out loud."

"Okay, yeah. He was a dick. At least it only took two dates for you to find out."

Ariel fidgeted in her seat. "Do you have something for me to do? I need to get my head back on straight."

After a moment of thought, Winter perked up. "You know what? Yes. Let's go set up a fake account on Wandering Hearts."

Ariel blinked and fixed her with a blank stare. "The app you warned me to stay away from? Winter, I'm a little chafed, but I'm not desperate."

"Not saying that. But you *are* interested in becoming an investigator. Or is that no longer in the cards?"

Ariel's bubbly manner returned in a heartbeat. "Okay, Boss. You have my attention. What are we looking for, and how does a sketchy dating app figure into our work?"

Winter suspected her assistant would jump at the chance to be part of an investigation. Motioning toward her office, she let Ariel precede her and get settled in a client chair. Collecting her messenger bag and mocha, Winter joined her and started the process to establish a profile on the app.

She and Ariel had only traded a few ideas for profile names when Kline came in through the front door, lugging a bag from a hardware store and a short length of black ABS pipe.

Having one profile will let us explore the app's community and

user base. Having two profiles would make that even easier—
especially if one of those profiles was a man's.

Before Winter could work up the courage to ask Kline, Ariel beat her to the punch.

"Hey, grizzly bear. Get your butt over here. Our boss has an assignment for us."

Winter winced. That was Ariel, as subtle as a speeding locomotive.

She waited as a frowning Kline set his burdens down by the still-unfinished sink.

He took his time, crossing the room like a tentative crab before stopping at Winter's office door. "What's the pit bull going on about?"

Winter sighed. "Children, play nice, or the teacher's putting you both in the corner."

That had the effect of encouraging Kline to call Ariel "a Rottweiler," which the young woman announced would be her new dating profile name.

"But not on this app. I'm going to use it on all my social media, though. Thanks, papa bear."

Kline staggered back a step and stared at Winter, his gaze revealing some kind of distress.

"You okay there, Kline?"

Nodding, he shuffled forward and settled himself into the chair beside Ariel. "Just a little touch of heartburn. Too much coffee this morning, I guess."

Winter knew that feeling. It didn't stop her from enjoying her mochas, though.

"Okay, you two. I need help with an investigation. This dating app is designed for people who want to cheat on their spouses, and it looks like a murderer is using the user base to select victims. We're going to build two fake profiles to try and lure them out."

Kline's wrinkled face remained as still as a statue. "Isn't

this the kind of thing your husband or the police should be doing? Sounds like we're trying to get between the law and a killer."

"We're not crossing any lines of legality here, and Detective Davenport will happily accept whatever helpful information I can give him. I just need you and Ariel to give me some suggestions for our make-believe cheaters."

"What's stopping you from making it up on your own?"

She did her best not to adopt a patronizing tone. "If I did it all myself, I could use similar phrasing or some other detail that might tip off the killer. I just need a few suggestions from you, not a life history."

"I'd rather have a root canal."

Ariel smacked his arm. "Aw, come on. You'll be helping to stop a killer. Isn't that enough to get you out from under that sink?"

He folded his arms, a hard line across his lips. "I don't want nobody knowin' nothin' about me."

"They won't. I'll be managing everything to do with the app. You won't have to lift a finger, and it won't even be you, really, not either of you. Just ideas you help me come up with."

Ariel nodded. "I'm game."

The older man sitting beside her assistant scratched his stubbly beard. "If it helps you, all right. But don't expect me to go meetin' no women or dressin' fancy in a tie. I don't own ties."

Relieved she'd talked her team into her caper, Winter began setting up the new accounts using throwaway email addresses.

She populated the profiles with details offered by Ariel and Kline, like their favorite hobbies and foods. Ariel was easier to get information from, and her long list of likes and dislikes added to the believability of her profile. Kline was about as forthcoming as a turnip.

Winter filled in his details with what she knew about her husband. Kline's older age coupled with Noah's likes and dislikes would make a compelling combination. Or so she hoped.

She made up their sexual preferences, hoping to entice the killer with the kinkiest interests she could imagine. Every profile she'd reviewed on the app had been several flavors removed from what she would call "vanilla."

Ariel's contributions included a name for the female profile. "Let's go with Terrier."

For the male profile, Winter had to pull teeth to get anything from Kline, and finally made an executive decision to use "Grizzly Bear."

"What about bios?" Ariel wriggled in her seat as they got to the meat of the profile setup. "We should come up with some really juicy ones."

"One step ahead of you there, but this is where I need your help the most. I looked at the victims' profiles and saw that both men made it clear they only wanted a fling. Terry Abbott said he needed to get something out of his system and that it would be 'a onetime thing, no strings attached.'"

"Yuck. If he wasn't a murder victim, I'd hate him."

"You're going to love Ernst Wald's bio, then." Winter opened a new tab and brought up the profile. Kline and Ariel huddled in to read it.

The old man scoffed and leaned away from the desk.

Ariel stifled a laugh. "He wishes he 'didn't have to do this?' News flash, jerk-face, you don't. Or you didn't, but there you go. Looks like professing devotion to a spouse is the common theme, so how do we help?"

Winter sat back and smiled. "First, you get a gold star for

spotting the link. Second, we need to come up with two novel but dissimilar ways of stating the same idea for these profiles. Terrier and Grizzly both need to express devotion for a spouse."

With a shake of his head, Kline headed for the door. "Ain't nothin' I can say that'll help you express something like that."

Ariel stopped him with a hand on his arm. "C'mon, grizzly bear. Just give us one word. Something that says 'forever' for you, or 'eternal love.'"

He glanced at her hand on his arm and covered it with his own, like Winter had seen Grampa Jack do so many times. Then, gently, Kline drew Ariel's fingers aside and stepped out of her grasp. "Can't say I'm familiar with things like that, I'm afraid. You and the boss'll do fine, I'm sure. I'm gonna get back to my plumbing now."

With that, he left the office, shutting the door behind him. Ariel spun to face Winter, her mouth drawn into a remorseful frown. "Sorry about that. I didn't know…"

"Neither did I, but that's Kline for you. He keeps everything under wraps. Let's finish these up and see where it gets us."

After a bit more brainstorming, they came up with "a desire for more than the usual" for Terrier's profile and "the freedom to be myself" for Grizzly's. In each case, they'd made sure to previously express "undying love" or "strong commitment" for the fictitious users' spouses.

With just a few keystrokes and following confirmation links sent to a pair of throwaway email addresses, Winter had the profiles ready to receive DMs.

Ariel checked out her profile on the computer. "So how long will it take?"

"Who knows?" Winter finished clicking on the agreement to publish section. "If the killer's watching for new profiles, we might…"

"Holy crap." Ariel gawked at the screen. "We're already getting hits."

"Terrier's the popular one, but G. B.'s had two 'likes' and one DM asking for a photo."

Ariel giggled as a ringing phone filled the outer office. "Don't tell me what they're saying. I don't want to eat my words about being desperate."

Winter watched the messages come in and eventually taper off to a trickle. She thought about the plan she and Noah had discussed, about using these profiles to lure out the killer.

She clicked through to the first user to message Ariel's profile and closed the message just as quickly.

I really didn't need to see that.

Almost every message she opened was more of the same —offering up unsolicited evidence of the user's arousal along with requests for proof that Terrier could play fetch. Winter gave up when she got to the one asking about costume play in the bedroom and whether ice cream was allowed between the sheets.

16

Winter waited as Noah reviewed the profiles she'd made for Kline and Ariel on her tablet. She warned him of what the messages they'd received contained, and he paused all of two seconds before opening the first of them.

"Remind me to tell you about the time I joined the Marine Corps. Takes a lot more than a dick pic to turn my stomach."

They both laughed, and Winter was again reminded of just how content she felt in Noah's presence. Even with the knowledge that someone might be watching them, she was comforted.

Noah thumbed through another message, this one sent to Grizzly Bear's profile. "Looks like maybe a handful each are asking for face photos, and the senders included some of theirs. We can reverse image search them."

"Already done, cowboy. I confirmed proof of life for each profile that sent a photograph and requested one in return. I asked Kline and Ariel for headshots we could use, with digital modifications, and they both okayed it."

"And you told them this could be dangerous, right?" Noah

lifted his beer from the coffee table. "They know what they signed on for?"

Winter tucked her knees under her. "They know, and Ariel's gung ho to help modify the images. She always wanted to be a police officer, so this is a dream gig for her."

Noah sipped his beer. "'I've become fodder for a serial killer.' Not exactly what I'd call a dream gig."

Winter rubbed her hand along his shoulder. "Does Falkner think there're going to be more murders? What have the clones and Eve come up with so far?"

"Nothing they're telling me about. Eve's been out of the office since yesterday, and the clones…Cooper and Bevin, dang it. I should use their names. Even if we don't ever talk."

"So you're just at your desk all day? By yourself?"

"I have Pokey to keep me company. But yeah, Falkner just has me doing more of what you did today. Running backgrounds on profiles and confirming proof of life. I found three bots today, though, so that's three profiles we can cross off the suspect list."

"Only nine thousand nine hundred and ninety-seven to go. What about those gold charms? I got so wrapped up in the profiles and messages, I didn't get a chance to make any calls today."

Noah took a swig of his beer and put his feet on the coffee table. "Cooper and Bevin are still on that. It's killing me to feel so useless."

Winter set the tablet aside. She hated hearing the defeat in her husband's voice. That wasn't him. He'd always loved chasing down leads and facts in a case. She could imagine how grueling sitting behind a computer for hours was for him. She'd hated that part of her job with the Bureau.

She scrubbed her face, chasing away her fatigue in an effort to focus. "We know the two victims cheated on their spouses. This could be some religious zealot angry that the sanctity of marriage has been defiled." She trembled as thoughts of The Preacher resurfaced.

Noah finished his beer and set the bottle down. "For me, stabbing the victims' hearts is a significant act of rage and, as you pointed out, likely means the killer knew them."

"I need to follow up with Betty Anne from the grocery store chain."

Noah sat up. "I wish I could do more than sit at a desk, but I'm trapped."

She leaned on his shoulder, wrapping her arms around him. "You could always drive me around to jewelry stores and pretend you're shopping while I ask about that broken heart charm."

"I love it when you're devious, but showing my face in those stores probably isn't a good idea. Just in case one of them is our killer's source for the charms. Video footage showing me there, with you, off duty…that won't look good in a courtroom."

"So you want me to check out the shitload of jewelry stores by myself. With a credit card in my pocket."

Noah kissed her nose. "Maybe leave that at home."

17

The next morning, Winter sat at her desk, trying to reach Betty Anne at Gardner Grocery.

She'd been on hold for two minutes so far, enjoying the Muzak Otis Gardner saw fit to torture callers with. After another four minutes, during which she scrolled through messages sent to her fake profiles on Wandering Hearts, she gave up on reaching Betty Anne by phone.

I'll just make a surprise visit while I'm out visiting jewelry stores.

Ariel popped her head into Winter's office with a mocha in hand and a smile on her face. "How's our case coming? Any interesting DMs on that app?"

Winter collected the coffee with both hands. "Good to see you back on your feet, but please tell me your enthusiasm is strictly related to the case."

Her assistant put a hand to her shirt collar. "Winter Black, you wound me. As if I'd seriously go looking for a date there. Unless you spotted somebody I should be thinking about?" She rounded Winter's desk and checked out the latest profile her boss had been examining.

Winter tapped the screen, a mixture of a grin and grimace on her face. "This one."

"He's cute, but I'm not sure I want to know what...pony play is. Nope, don't tell me."

She was back around Winter's desk and making a beeline for her own before Winter could stop herself from laughing. "It's just another flavor of ice cream. Nobody's telling you to buy it."

"Hey, I don't judge."

Still chuckling, Winter packed up her tablet and gathered her things. It was time to hit the streets and see what she could find out about those gold charms.

And hopefully get a few more words in with Betty Anne Rose-Thomas.

Ariel cocked an eyebrow as Winter passed her desk on the way out. "You're not leaving me here alone with the grizzly bear, are you?"

"Hey," Kline growled, still on his back beneath the sink, "I heard that."

Winter rolled her eyes. "Didn't I tell you to play nice? Both of you?"

Her contractor grumbled some more and banged a wrench against the sink, but Winter couldn't tell if he was expressing his mood or making an adjustment to the pipes. Ariel hunched over her desk, covering her whisper with a hand. "Seriously, take me with you."

Winter debated how much she should share with her assistant. Ariel wanted to explore investigation as a career, and canvassing jewelers would be easier with two of them. But Winter couldn't think clearly with Ariel chattering away beside her.

"Not this time. I need to canvass the stores first, get the lay of the land. If I need to make a repeat trip to any of them, I'll bring you along."

Ariel deflated a bit but perked up as Winter brought out her phone and opened the photo Noah sent her.

"The two victims were found with this gold charm." She turned the phone for her assistant to see.

Ariel peered at the image. "That's new. The ones I know are the kind you share with a friend or lover. Half a heart that fits with the other half, like puzzle pieces. Who would wear a charm of a broken heart?"

"I'm sure it can't be that uncommon. Plenty of people focus on the sad and morbid aspects of life. Goths and emos aren't anything new."

Ariel sat back in her chair. "I could see those types wearing costume pieces, but that looks like real gold. Did Noah say if it was or not?"

"No, he only had the photo to go on. Why do you think the type of metal matters?"

"I worked in a jewelry store right out of high school, remember? It was on my résumé."

Winter never bothered to tell Ariel she couldn't remember what she had for breakfast, let alone something on a résumé she read weeks ago. "Do you think someone there might know where these charms came from?"

Ariel shrugged. "You might get a list of shops that sell that specific piece. All stores have software that tracks sales and shipments. The trick is finding the store where the unsub bought them. Some places deal in all cash and ask no questions, if you know what I mean. And these days, a lot of jewelry is purchased online. That would take a lifetime to track."

Winter knew all too well what she was up against. The killer had already proven themselves clever enough to avoid leaving a trace at either scene.

They probably bought several of these charms in preparation for their killing spree.

"Should I tell any callers you're out of the office today?" Ariel waited for Winter's reply. "I mean, if you're going to hit local jewelry stores all day, you won't have time to meet with new clients."

"What makes you think I'm going to any jewelry stores?"

Ariel chuckled. "You wouldn't have asked if you weren't considering it. I know you. You don't let things fester for long."

Before Winter could respond, Kline's deep grumble came to her from the kitchen area. "Gonna need one more pipe fitting, but I'll have the sink finished today if it kills me. Honest Abe."

"Thanks, Kline. Can I trust the two of you not to bite each other while I'm gone?"

"I won't if she don't."

Ariel scoffed. "Not even if I was starving. We'll hold things down for you here."

Winter headed for the door, draining the last of her mocha and dropping the cup in the trash before exiting.

On the street, she thought about where the case had taken her so far and what she and Noah might be up against.

She'd need to watch her step. One wrong move could land Noah in hot water with the Bureau or land them both in a murderer's crosshairs.

18

I scrolled angrily through the newest profiles, watching the numbers and names zipping up my screen in a blur. Winter Black had found my app. Not only that, she'd set up two profiles in a clumsy attempt to lure me out. Both profiles had gone up in quick succession from the same IP address. Neither featured a photograph, and the profile details couldn't have been more cobbled together.

Winter had been married for some time, I suspected, so of course she'd have trouble crafting a genuine-sounding profile for a dating app.

You've wasted your time, Ms. Black. I'm the one who baits the trap in this game.

It had worked twice so far, and I knew it would work again. After all, didn't I have a date with Kristine Tippett later tonight? We'd made plans to see a late-night showing at an art house cinema she liked. I'd visited the place yesterday to ensure the venue would suit my needs, and it couldn't have been more perfect.

Feeling renewed vigor for my task, I clicked over to

Winter's profile for "Grizzly Bear." An older gentleman, with "refined tastes" and "a knack for using his hands."

"Good god, can you possibly be less inspired? I thought you were an FBI agent once upon a time."

I quickly grew bored exploring "Grizzly's" tastes and interests, even though I did find some humor in how many messages his profile had received. So far, Winter had not sent any replies to his admirers.

For a moment, I toyed with the idea of doing so on her behalf. I had admin access to every user's DMs, and it would be so easy to send simpering replies from "Grizzly Bear." But then, Winter would know I was watching her. She might not be able to write a compelling profile description, but she wasn't an idiot.

Nobody who survived the horrors of Justin Black, and took him down in the end, could be called stupid.

I scrolled over to her profile for "Terrier" next. Like "Grizzly Bear," no picture had been posted at first. But two reply messages included the image of a gleeful brunette with ringlets hanging to her shoulders and a smile that could probably sell toothpaste.

I didn't recognize the woman, but I knew a doctored photo when I saw one. It was probably a stock image, or maybe one from Winter's high school yearbook. Either way, I'd find out.

My spyware gave me the IP address of every user on Wandering Hearts. A simple collating program I'd written provided me with a running list of all users based on zip code. That, plus my GPS tracker, let me watch Winter move around the city whenever she carried my app with her.

So far, I'd only learned that she lived in the Destiny Bluff subdivision and had an office downtown.

And she loves that coffee shop down the street from her office. She's been there twice today already.

Going to Winter's website again, I clicked on the tab marked *Staff*. I couldn't contain my little bubble of excitement. The brunette's photograph was a modified image of Ariel Joyner, the Executive Assistant for Black Investigations.

Now I could start thinking about how I'd remove Winter's troublesome nose from the picture.

And the rest of her along with it.

But first things first. I had to get to work and then get ready for my date tonight. I had no doubt KT would provide me ample entertainment when I slid a knife into her chest and carved her cheating heart to pieces.

Maybe I'd even take it out of her body and slice it in two, so when she was found, everyone would know why she'd been killed.

Would that be going too far, though? Too much and too soon?

The police had begun investigating my app, as well, and so had the *actual* FBI—not just their former agent turned private investigator.

It wouldn't be long before law enforcement managed to break through the protections I'd built around myself. A subpoena would compel service providers to turn over their records, and eventually, some clever agent would find the trail that led to me.

The Tor network could only be counted on to shield me for so long. I'd always known I'd have to relocate, but I had plans in place for that. My mother's house in Los Angeles would still suffice as a waypoint on my journey before I found my next killing ground.

Where would I go? Boston? Or maybe I'd try to track down Simon in Taiwan. Could I find a way to live there and stay hidden as easily as I could in this country? Doubtful, and killing Simon would make any attempts at concealing myself even harder.

I glanced around my apartment, at the monitors and computer towers I'd need to pack up someday soon. They were my true lair. The real me didn't even exist in the living world anymore. What people saw of me was merely what I allowed them to see—a ghost of an image. A fleeting charade I used to conceal my authentic self from view.

I could play the damsel in distress, as I'd done for Terry. I could play the wounded, longing widow, as I'd done for Ernst.

Who would I be when I took Winter Black's heart from her chest? Who would I be for Kristine tonight?

Spinning my chair around, I jumped to my feet and headed for my closet. My costumes hung in groups, arranged by color. An armada of options to choose from as I prepared myself for battle with the world's most unfaithful and fickle hearts.

Dear Kristine, are you feeling blue tonight? Maybe violet? What about a deep bloodred?

19

A warm breeze caressed Winter's face as she walked into the All Is Gold jewelry store.

Glass display cases on pedestals adorned the floor. Others hung on the walls, showcasing the fabulous jewelry offered. Winter wasn't a glitzy woman, and bling didn't usually excite her, but the exceptional display of her aquamarine birthstone set in a chunky gold band did tempt her. Just a little.

It's only been a week since my birthday, and Noah wouldn't say anything if I brought home a little something for myself.

"Can I help you?"

The feminine voice belonged to a leggy brunette with inquisitive brown eyes, the cut of her slim blue dress highlighting her curves. Winter couldn't imagine wearing something so revealing at work.

The attendant stood behind a stunning array of gemstones that added to her allure, waiting with her gloved hands neatly folded on the glass top of the case.

"Hello." Winter approached the counter. "I was looking for some information on a gold charm." She removed her phone from her messenger bag's side pocket while admiring the white gloves. "What are those for?"

The woman waved to the sparkling diamond watches and sapphire bracelets in a glass case. "We have to wear them to handle the jewelry. To prevent smudging."

Winter opened her phone and found the picture Noah had sent her. She placed the device on the counter with the image showing on the screen. "I wanted to know if you've sold charms like this lately."

The pretty brunette leaned over, her hair falling over her shoulders as she studied the picture. She snickered and glanced up. "We don't get any orders for this particular charm in our store. Our clientele tends to shop from shelves a little bit higher than where you'd find that thing."

"Does that mean it's not real gold?" Winter squinted at the photo, remembering what Ariel had said.

The shop clerk shook her head. "No, it probably is real, but not solid. I'd expect a stamped nickel core covered in plate, or maybe ten karat."

"What's the difference?"

The clerk smiled and lowered her eyes, as if offering Winter an apology. "It's a costume piece, the kind of thing you'd find at a discount retailer. Those charms are popular with people who are into the new divorce-party craze. And with teenagers."

Winter had heard of such events and wondered how anybody could think to celebrate the end of a marriage. Then again, she had to admit that not every marriage was like her and Noah's.

"So you've never sold anything like this?"

"No. We only carry authentic merchandise. Genuine gold, silver, and platinum. If you're looking for something…" She tapped her lips. "How do I say this? At a lower price point, I can suggest some retailers online. Dozens sell charms like this."

"Dozens?" Considering the volume of internet stores offering the gem, tracking the jewelry might be impossible. She'd need resources akin to the FBI's to get all the invoices from such places.

The clerk leaned across the counter. "Can I ask what this is about?"

Winter put her phone away and pulled a business card from another pocket in her bag. "I'm looking into this for a client. Winter Black of Black Investigations. I'd appreciate it if you'd let me know whether anyone does happen to come in here requesting that charm."

The woman accepted the card. "I'm Cassie. Cassie Pattell, but I doubt we'll ever get anyone wanting something like that. Our clients are more about buying rings to go on wedding fingers, not celebrating divorces."

"Ah, yeah, I can understand that." Winter pointed at her card. "I'd still appreciate a call if you hear any more about that charm or if anyone comes in asking for it."

She left the store, grateful she didn't have to navigate the shark-infested dating waters like Ariel. Having someone to go home to—someone she trusted with her life—was a gift. It made her question what the victims had wanted so badly that they'd risked everything.

And they paid that price, in full, while getting absolutely nothing in return.

20

An overly buttery aroma of popcorn permeated the air as I made my way through the Marquee Art House Theater, which was darker than the night outside. Images of Winter Black and her assistant rampaged through my head. I did my best to ignore the nagging thoughts and concentrate on why I'd come to this place.

Kristine wanted to meet here to "try something new." She liked the idea of having a tryst in a public place. I hated the request but loved her choice of location. This little cinema was always minimally attended, and it provided a perfect getaway route.

Plus, they had weekly showings of a gory slasher flick, full of screams that would cover up any noise Kristine might make when I pierced her cheating heart.

I'd bought a ticket for an earlier showing that evening and spent the break between screenings in the bathroom. As the time for Kristine's arrival drew near, I found a seat at the back of the theater and waited. I folded my gloved hands over my knee.

She would be here soon.

Being built inside an old department store building, this theater had access doors in odd places, including the one I'd use to escape. My exit stood at the bottom of the stairs to my right and would take me to the lobby. Those steps ran beside the shallow tiers of seating and were only visible to people in the top three rows.

Thankfully, nobody was in attendance tonight except for me.

The screen came to life with obnoxiously loud trailers. The cacophony of noise would serve my purpose beautifully.

For a moment, I imagined a future where I'd forgiven Simon for his treachery, even after I'd made a home for us with my hard-earned income. A world where all my former lovers were forgiven for their inability to stay true.

My first girlfriend, Dani, had literally fled from the apartment I'd rented for us as a surprise six-month anniversary gift. I moved her stuff from the bedroom she rented in a house she shared with classmates while she was busy studying and taking final exams.

I spent the day, staying home from work and using sick time to do it, to pack, load, and move boxes of her clothes and possessions. I even bought her all new bath towels and toiletries. All fresh and clean and waiting for her arrival.

She'd screamed at me when she came in, demanding to know what I'd done with her things. When I showed her, she shouted some more, accusing me of being abusive and controlling.

My calls went unanswered that night and for the rest of the week. On a Thursday, I received an envelope in the mail with a return address from the local superior court containing a restraining order.

A second letter, with a return address from a legal firm, instructed me to vacate the property for a period of twenty-four hours so Dani could "safely collect" her possessions.

She left the towels and toiletries behind.

A few days later, I got another letter, from her this time. She accused me of wanting to "sculpt" her life and said she never wanted to see me again. As I watched a trailer for a film about metal workers, I fantasized about setting Dani's things on fire and watching them all burn with her at the center.

As if my love and devotion were some perverse attempt at controlling her. Abuse? She has no idea what abuse is.

A figure entered my row, and I startled, pulling my legs in to make room.

"Hi, Alex."

Lowering my feet to the floor, I let my knee brush against Kristine's pant leg. She wore a perfect outfit for what I had planned. Black slacks under a dark floral print blouse and a jacket.

The blood wouldn't be noticeable to anyone at first. It was almost like she knew she was going to die and wanted to make my job easier.

How thoughtful, Kristine. But you're still here to cheat and throw away your wife's devotion as if it were trash.

Tonight, I'd be turning that trash into treasure.

She settled into the seat beside me and leaned over the armrest to place a kiss on my neck, all soft lips and warm breath. A shudder raced through me, and my hand flew into my coat pocket for the knife.

"I'm so glad you made it." She made a noise in her throat like the purr of a kitten ready for a bowl of fresh cream.

I said nothing and simply let her keep touching me as my hands rested in my lap to conceal the knife I now held. She continued kissing my neck, her mouth trailing up to my ear.

"I'm glad no one else came to see the show. I thought this was better than a motel."

Pictures I'd seen online of Kristine, her wife, and her dog

lingered in my head as I eased my hands upward. My anger grew as I considered her betrayal.

When she moaned against my neck, I smiled. That would end soon enough. The movie had started, and the soundtrack of blaring heavy metal music would give me the perfect cover.

I glanced at the screen. The credits were drawing to a close, the music dropping to a tamer rhythm.

I kissed Kristine's neck, anticipation tingling my fingertips as the film's first screams burst through the speakers and the opening murder scene began. I watched from the corner of my eye, waiting for my moment.

A group of teenagers on a roller coaster screamed as the cart they were in roared along its tracks at ridiculous speed. Save for a full moon, the sky above them was black as pitch. Below the terrified teens, a clown wearing bloodred face paint cackled like a maniac and pulled a lever.

The roller coaster cart sped faster, going downhill. Sparks flew, and metal screeched against metal. The young victims screamed again as the camera zoomed in on their gaping mouths and their wide, terrified eyes.

I lifted my hand from my lap, collecting the knife. Still kissing Kristine's slender neck, I used my other hand to direct her chin upward, to ensure she couldn't see the blade.

But her eyes were closed anyway. She was moaning softly. I placed a kiss below her collar.

Before plunging the blade, I slipped my hand over her chin to cover her mouth and looked back to the screen.

A thunderous beat erupted from the speakers as images of the teenagers' shredded bodies flooded the screen. The cart had flown from the tracks, and they'd all been flung to the ground, tumbling and sliding across the pavement as the clown waited for them with a knife in his hand.

The killer stalked toward one of the teens, who lay

panting and bloody, holding up his hands as if he might stop the inevitable.

The clown reared back, poising his knife against the blackened sky above. Now was my chance. I drove my blade in just as the clown struck, eliciting a scream from his first victim.

Kristine's eyes popped open and bulged with terror when I thrust the knife into her cheating heart.

She vibrated in the seat as I covered her body with mine, mimicking the actions of a lover too impatient to wait for a more private venue. The rush of her blood warmed my wrist, pouring over my gloved hand. I felt the life ebbing from her like a tide retreating from the shore, just as Dani retreated from me, forever to remain adrift without the grounding support I had so freely and willingly provided.

But whose feet are still on the ground, Dani?

I'd bet anything that Dani was struggling to succeed in life, just like Simon would have if he hadn't profited from my ideas and fled with his plunder like a common thief.

Speaking of struggling, Kristine had gone limp beneath me. I glanced over my shoulder. The clown had finished off all four of his initial victims. He wandered to a popcorn machine and filled a bag for himself.

After I returned the knife to my jacket pocket, I removed my wet gloves and replaced them with a fresh pair from the other pocket. The tainted ones took their place. I'd dispose of them later.

Smears of Kristine's blood stained my blouse, but my jacket would hide them while I left the theater. Lots of people walked out of flicks. No one would notice a patron leaving early.

Before I left, I reverently placed a charm on Kristine's forehead. She now lay slumped back in her seat, the cheater's mark glinting above her brow.

In the lobby, a group of young people lingered at the popcorn counter. A man exited the restroom while another stepped around him to go in. I saw all this in my peripheral vision, as I kept my eyes on the stained carpet. On the street, I breathed in the night air. Hints of exhaust, blended with the fading aroma of popcorn, had me aching for an escape far away from the city.

I would have to leave town soon. But first, I had another cheater to kill, and then an irritating problem to solve…one that could potentially follow me wherever I tried to hide.

That problem's name was Winter Black.

21

Noah's edginess was getting the better of him as he sat in the Austin VCU conference room. He stared out the glass wall into the hallway, watching other agents carrying folders and tablets, seemingly busy with assignments. He envied their frenzied activity. Why did he feel like a slow-moving blue whale in an office of mako sharks?

Across the table, Agent Gallegos scrolled through notes on his iPad. Eve sat to Noah's left, assessing him with her skeptical gaze. He knew that look. Eve was worried.

"How's Winter's grandmother? You haven't mentioned her lately." Eve's eyes scoured his face. "Everything okay?"

Noah ran his finger along the rim of the coffee cup before him. "Beth's doing well. Getting better every day. Getting the diagnosis was tough, but so's Beth."

SSA Falkner marched into the conference room. The red on the man's cheeks alerted Noah that whatever had hastened his boss's footsteps wasn't good. Weston only moved quickly when time was of the essence. In their job, that meant a killer was on the loose.

"We have another stabbing victim. M.O. appears to match

Terry Abbott and Ernst Wald, but this one's a woman." He set his tablet on the conference room table. "She was found in the Marquee Art Theater, one of those little art house spots downtown. Only one person had a ticket for the show, and that was the victim, which means the killer either snuck in or was already inside."

Shit. If the killer snuck in, the chance of them having avoided any CCTV cameras was high. "Security cameras?"

Falkner frowned. "Working on it. Theater staff have already been questioned, as have employees who weren't on shift last night. So far, their alibis are good. Police have begun tracking down anyone who attended the other showings around then. We have a limited pool of suspects, but that's still going to take time." He picked up his tablet and swiped across the screen.

An image shined on the board behind his head. The logo for Wandering Hearts—a heart-shaped balloon with a string on it floating away.

"The victim's name is Kristine Tippett. She was twenty-seven, married to her wife of two years, and maintained a profile on this app. Like the other two dead men, she was found with a broken heart charm on her forehead."

"That changes things." Agent Gallegos jabbed the air with his tablet pen. "We thought we were dealing with a woman before. This murder means we could have a male unsub or a team."

"All this means is our killer doesn't discriminate." Falkner gestured at the board behind him. "Like I said, PD are canvassing possible suspects from among the theater attendees and staff. I want all our attention focused on Wandering Hearts. Cyber has yet to track the source for the app."

Noah raised a hand. "Sir, we don't have hosting or Who Is data yet?"

"Negative on both, Agent Dalton. Nothing reliable anyway. Whoever's behind this thing, they're bouncing around the Tor network. Every interaction between users is routed through the dark web."

It was at times like this when Noah missed his former teammate, the prickly but digitally brilliant Sun Ming. He wouldn't have coffee with her, but he'd damn sure take one of her offhand announcements that she'd found a new lead for them. "So we can't even confirm if the app host is involved in the murders or if one of the users is exploiting the app's secrecy to commit these crimes."

Falkner nodded. "Correct. And that brings me to another point. Nobody in this room should assume we're only looking for one person. The app and murders are connected, but we can't say for certain whether that means one person or a pair, or even a team, is involved."

The ramifications hit Noah in the chest. They could be searching for a whole squad of killers, all using the same interface to select and lure victims, perhaps doing so without the actual app host's awareness.

Eve must have been thinking along the same lines. She stabbed a pen at the screen. "Sir, is it possible that whoever's behind the app isn't aware their users are being targeted this way?"

"That's a possibility."

"But so far, we only have victims in the Austin area. Nothing in other states to indicate this is a wider effort?"

The SSA shook his head. "Thankfully, no. From what we've learned, the app is only available to Austin residents. Whoever's behind it, they've built a sophisticated vetting system that can defeat attempts to download the app outside of certain zip codes."

Eve sat back in her chair, her lips pressed into a slight grimace. "That's going to give Cyber something to do, but we're limited to scrolling the victims' Facebook feeds, aren't we?"

"That one and others. Kristine Tippett was active on several platforms, apparently trying to make a name for herself as a singer and songwriter. See what you can dig up there."

"What about the media?"

Weston sighed and rested his fists on the table. "Austin PD released Wald's and Abbott's names to the press. We should assume Tippett will be released soon, so prepare for a media onslaught. You know the drill. We are investigating all leads and will provide an update the minute we have one."

22

Winter had spent a large part of her day picking up
paperwork from small-time lawyers who would rather pay
her to serve notices and summons than maintain a paralegal
in-house. It wasn't exciting work.

*But it keeps the lights on, and right now, that has to be reason
enough to do this job.*

After multiple trips around the city, she'd finally managed
a break to visit Gardner Grocery and talk to Betty Anne
again. All she got for her trouble was reassurance that the
woman planned to retire in four days, and had, in fact,
already revealed those plans to Otis Gardner himself.

*"He offered to buy me a going away present, something to
remember the job. I told him the pension checks would be just fine
and not to trouble himself."*

Winter probed the woman's plans for her retirement as
best she could without appearing too interested. Her earlier
suspicions about Betty Anne being the killer were quickly
dashed when she described the quilting circle she belonged
to for the past year and a half.

"We meet every night, just a bunch of us who live alone but are

still active and looking for social opportunities. I'm the last of us to retire, and we're all planning a trip to Europe next month."

Being a quilter didn't exonerate anyone from also being a murderer, but in Betty Anne's case, her hobby provided a solid alibi.

Winter had wanted to press the secretary further, but Gardner had come out and interrupted their conversation. Beyond a polite request that she please exit the premises, he'd had no pleasant words to share.

She made two more stops at jewelers, asking about the broken heart charm, and got two more versions of the narrative Cassie Pattell from All Is Gold had given her.

"That charm is gross. People buy the things mostly online and give them out as a party favor at their divorce or break-up celebrations."

"I've never sold one, but I've seen it before. My wife put it in my stocking last Christmas. I thought it was a joke until the divorce papers arrived after New Year's."

Winter asked if the man's ex was still in the area.

"She and her fiancé live here. He earns a little more than jewelry counter wages, so I don't have to worry about running into them unless I'm picking up night work ushering at the opera."

And so went the day, until at last, Winter was back at her own desk, listening to Kline work in the kitchen while she sifted through emails and the list of calls to return that Ariel had given her when she walked in.

The bubbly assistant sitting at her desk in the main office caught Winter's eye with the wave of a hand. "Date night returns. Any chance I can take off a little before five to get ready?"

"New guy this time, I'm guessing?"

"Yes. His name's Robert. We're meeting for cocktails and tapas at a cool rooftop spot. It used to be a sporting goods store with golfing lanes up there. They replaced all the nets and fences, so you get a great view of the skyline."

Winter waved her off. "Go ahead. I'll manage anything that comes in."

"Thanks, Boss! I'll text when I get there and when I leave, and I'll call when I'm back home. Shouldn't be later than nine o'clock." With a little salute, Ariel scooped up her bag and jacket, and she was out the door in under a minute.

Kline's shuffling form emerged from the kitchen area. He'd finished the sink, as promised, and had spent much of the day ensuring none of the plumbing leaked and, when it did, making the needed repairs.

He worked slowly—as slowly as he moved it seemed—but he got the job done.

"You're all set back there. You let the pit bull off her leash early again, I see. Sure that's a good idea?"

"Kline, please stop calling her that. I don't remember her using the words 'grizzly' or 'bear' before she left. In fact, I think she might have even used your name."

He hefted a wrench in one hand and wiped at the tool with a rag. "That's fair. Just don't like how she's always stepping out early. But it's your store. You run the place however it suits you."

Winter put a hand to her brow in a comical salute, which Kline returned, complete with an effort at standing at attention. As he held the wrench against his shoulder like it were a rifle, she couldn't help but snort at the man's silly stance.

He winked. "Glad I can still make you laugh at least. Guess I'll be off, too, unless you want me to stick around."

"Go for it. I'll be fine."

He hesitated before nodding and retrieving his tool kit from the kitchen. Once he reached the door, he turned and waved at her before exiting into the breezy Austin evening.

Returning her attention to the emails open on her laptop, Winter's mood sank. Was this what her life amounted to now?

She'd spent the day speeding from errand to errand, the worry that her brother's cultish fan club was spying on her lingering constantly under the surface.

Justin's influence on her life hadn't ended with his capture, and she'd grown damn tired of the power he still held over her. Potential hidden cameras were a persistent buzzing in her brain. Winter felt her attention split between concentrating on the case in front of her and stressing about who might be watching her work.

With a sigh, Winter closed her laptop, telling herself the emails could wait. Reading and replying to client inquiries was vital to her continued success as a P.I., but it also wore on her.

The more immediate and exciting task of tracking a killer was all she could think about anyway.

Winter pulled out her tablet and opened Wandering Hearts, determined not to let her private concerns color her efforts. When she logged in to Ariel's profile, she goggled at the number of messages she'd received. It would take ages to sift through them, and they were still coming in.

The notification icon showed a counter that climbed from two hundred and fifty likes and ten DMs up to two hundred and ninety-six likes and over two dozen DMs.

And now we're at three hundred and sixteen likes. Yikes.

She opened the most recent message, from a user with the name *unbreakmyheart2.*

See you're new here. Meet up sometime soon? I know all the best places in town.

The user's profile was bare-bones, with links to blurred-out images. Their bio listed gender as "prefer not to state" and included a tagline.

Message me with your deepest desires to see my images.

Winter passed and checked the message that arrived. It was more to the point, and included a photograph from the sender, which he identified as "proof that I mean what I say."

No doubt, buddy. If you're telling me you're a dick.

Other messages were more of the same. Most of the ones she opened repeated the refrain of what the sender wanted to do, not so much with but *to* Ariel. The additional downside was that none of the messages stood out, and Winter's ability had apparently chosen to take the night off.

Not a single profile emitted any kind of red glow.

If she and Noah were going to track the killer through the app, it would take more computer skills than either of them possessed. She needed a quick way to sort the text of all the messages she'd received and find patterns.

Sinking back into her chair, she stretched her legs under her desk.

Maybe it was time to accept she needed the Bureau's resources.

No, that would mean admitting defeat. Winter and Noah would either crack the case, or the Bureau would figure it out without her direct help. Whatever transpired, she and Noah would remain free to determine their own fates and futures—together.

Growing weary of discovering just how many men seemed to equate their identities with their anatomy, Winter exited the app and logged back in on Kline's profile. She wasn't surprised by the few messages he'd received. Terrier was a twentysomething female, swimming in an ocean of indiscriminate men. Grizzly Bear was an older man in a tiny pool of women, most of them younger than him.

He had three messages total.

The most recent one was unmistakably familiar.

See you're new here. Meet up sometime soon? I know all the best places in town.

The sender was the same, if using an alt account. Username *unbreakmyheart1* beckoned at the end of the message, hyperlinked to the app's messaging software.

Winter searched Ernst Wald's profile and scrolled through the users who had "liked" Wald's bio. Right there at the top, the first to like the profile, was username *unbreakmyheart1.*

She logged out of Grizzly Bear's profile and went back to Terrier's to double-check that the message from *unbreakmyheart2* was identical to the one sent to Grizzly Bear. Word for word, they matched. She clicked the link, opening the message software in Terrier's profile, and tapped out a reply.

Love to meet up. How does tomorrow night sound?

She waited nervously as the cursor blinked on the open message page.

A minute passed, then two. Winter worried she'd blown it, or that she'd been duped by a bot that probably spat out the same message to every profile on the app.

She was about to log off when a message pinged in Terrier's inbox.

Tomorrow is great. I'm free after 7. Cocktails at Magro's?

Ariel had gone to that restaurant with her last date. That Winter was receiving a message suggesting the spot didn't necessarily mean a connection existed, but she'd learned a long time ago not to dismiss supposed coincidences.

The app pinged again.

Want to meet?

Winter pumped a fist in the air. She'd caught a fish. All she had to do was find out who was on the other end of the hook.

She opened the Tracers app she kept on her computer,

ready to run down the IP address of *unbreakmyheart2.* She waited as the software chased down the router used by the messenger.

A map popped up on the software page. It would show the location of the server used to send the message.

The three dots, indicating the software was searching, blinked for several minutes.

Something's wrong. It never takes this long. I bet they're using a VPN. Even so, I should be able to find...

The map on her screen came to life, and a line appeared, connecting her computer in Austin to another in Ogden, Utah.

Winter blinked, not believing her eyes. Her profiles had explicitly called for anyone replying to be within the Austin area.

Another red line appeared on the map, going from Winter's computer in Austin to Boston.

Then another line appeared, connecting Austin to New Orleans.

Winter sat back in her chair, watching the lines crisscrossing the map on her screen. Whoever was behind the *unbreakmyheart* accounts was using an advanced roaming router and the Tor network to mask their IP address.

She'd seen similar programs used by hackers eager to penetrate government sites, but Wandering Hearts was not a federal operation with state secrets to protect.

Winter gaped at the growing array of lines on the tracing software map. The bouncing signal had worked its way through five states.

Though she had the beginnings of a reply typed out, she was considering whether to suggest a different location. If *unbreakmyheart* was the killer, they could have chosen Magro's because the establishment was familiar terrain. Winter knew better than to meet a killer on their home turf.

But where could she suggest that would give her and Noah an edge? They hadn't gone out to dinner or on a date in Austin more than a handful of times.

The app pinged again, alerting Winter to another message from *unbreakmyheart.*

Still breathing? I am.

Typing a quick reply that Magro's at seven thirty would be fine, Winter held her breath as the cursor blinked and a response came back.

That's perfect. Can't wait to find out what makes your heart beat.

Winter's fingers froze above her keyboard. She grabbed her phone and called Noah.

"I'm on my way home. What's up?"

"I'm still at the office but leaving now. I think the killer just sent me a message on Wandering Hearts."

23

I sat at my computer, entranced by the screen. It had been so easy to identify which profiles Winter Black was using to investigate me. The FBI had been trying to breach my security all week. They hadn't even discovered my IP address yet, but here was Winter Black, trading messages with me without any awareness.

And she wasn't the only one. Another device connected to her office address had downloaded the app recently and built a profile. It was pathetically simple, and the username was as banal as could be.

"John Allen. My, my, but aren't you an enticing creature. Barf."

It was probably Winter's husband offering to help her out. I'd done a little more digging into her history and learned she was married to an FBI agent named Noah Dalton. A man with a name as plain as that probably *would* come up with "John Allen" as an alias.

What a pair of idiots they are, thinking they can fool me.

I kept watching the mobile device that had left Winter's office. It was steadily moving away from the downtown area.

I added John Allen's profile to my list of favorites for later perusal and went back to trading messages with Winter on her Terrier profile.

She was still in her office.

While I waited for her reply, I scrolled through messages I'd received from the other users I'd flagged on the night I killed Ernst. Most were easy enough to ignore, but one caught my eye. A woman aching for excitement since her marriage had "lost its spark" and was only keeping her "housed but not loved."

The profile owner called herself *Miranda56* and confessed to still loving her husband, despite his inability to satisfy her in bed.

Oh, you idiot. As if sexual ability were any measure of the capacity for genuine love. I'll be doing your poor husband a favor by taking you out of his life.

Miranda56 wasn't online at the moment, so I just sent my standard opening message.

See you're new here. Meet up sometime soon? I know all the best places in town.

Finished, I went back to Terrier's profile to see if Winter had responded. Nothing new from her yet, but her device's IP address was in transit.

Looks like someone's going home.

I checked John Allen's device again and spotted it roaming a neighborhood on the other side of town, nowhere near Winter's home in Destiny Bluff.

So it wasn't her husband. Or probably wasn't. I couldn't be sure, of course, since he was an FBI agent.

Either way, Winter Black was clearly not going to leave me be, and she'd enlisted help to hunt me down.

For those reasons alone, she had to die.

Anyone with that level of devotion and commitment would be a difficult opponent to outwit. I could rely on my security to keep her out of my actual lair, but she'd demonstrated a desire to see things through.

So very like me. We probably would've been great friends if we'd met earlier in life. Before Simon took that last good piece of my heart and crushed it under his bootheel.

Once I was faced with the same withering reality that destroyed my mother—that cheaters and deceivers would always debase any genuine efforts at building love between two people—well, my fate was sealed. My course was set, and the road had brought me face-to-face with Winter Black.

A worse nemesis might have existed. If she'd actually been Dani, instead of just *looking* like her, I might've faltered in my next steps.

But killing Winter was always going to be my last move before I fled the Austin area for greener and safer pastures. My mother's home was still available to me in Los Angeles. I would relocate there and begin building a new network of trusted contacts, establishing myself as a clerk in some high-end boutique again.

Maybe I'd sell designer fashion on Rodeo Drive. I had a supply of my heart charms, purchased in bulk. I reached a gloved hand into their box, swirling my fingers through the little gold-plated trinkets.

My computer pinged with notifications as Winter agreed to meet at Magro's later.

One more fluttering insect about to be trapped in my web.

I sat back, proud of my accomplishment.

Winter's IP address vanished from my tracker—meaning she'd probably logged out or turned off her device. But just as fast, another message popped up from the app associated with the mobile device.

Would you want to have dinner sometime?

Really? A dinner date? I couldn't hold in my laughter. "Yeah, okay, grandpa, let's do dinner."

I typed out a reply.

If you're on the menu, maybe. What do you say?

It took a little time, but I got a message back.

That sounds okay. I guess.

I left it at that but made a mental note to pick up the conversation again soon. I needed to know who else, other than Winter Black, might be trying to trick me into revealing myself.

Several newer profiles had popped up, all with GPS data that confirmed they were set up by the FBI or Austin PD. Those were easy enough to ignore, though. Especially because none of them were directly linked to Winter Black.

I had a date with my nemesis soon, but I didn't have everything in place quite yet. First, I needed to throw Winter a curveball. I'd message her tomorrow morning, asking for a change of venue. I knew she had to be planning a stakeout of her own at Magro's, probably with her FBI husband providing backup.

But if I switched the time and location, and she still agreed to meet, I might be able to get her alone. And then we'd see who would be the predator and who would be the prey.

My money's on the spider who spun the web in the first place.

24

Winter somehow beat Noah home, which probably meant traffic was a mess. He'd been on the road when she called him from her office. She'd wanted him to be there already, so she wouldn't be in the house alone while a murderer possibly aware of her exact location roamed the streets.

Whoever the killer is, they connected my fake profiles to me. That means they're tracing IP addresses, which means they know where I live.

If she and Noah were right, and the killer had ties to Justin's cult, then that wasn't new information. But until now, it had only been speculation.

Trading messages with someone Winter felt certain was the killer put everything in a new perspective. Instead of hoping for a repeat of their evening from earlier in the week, she'd done nothing but pace the front room.

She hadn't even opened the wine yet, much less taken off her shoes or hung her messenger bag on the hook inside the door. She still had the strap over one shoulder.

Keys jingled outside, the front door cracked open, and Noah's face appeared.

"Hey, darlin'." He walked in, his tie askew and a coffee stain on his shirt.

"You look like hell." She stepped toward him but stopped when he looked her up and down, his face pinched with concern.

"And you look ready to run. What's going on?"

She told him about her exchanges on the app and about the date at Magro's. "I can't stop thinking about ways the murderer can track locations. I mean, I know they set up meetings with their victims, but they're pretty tech savvy, using VPNs and bouncing signals all over the place. It's making me paranoid. This whole case is just amplifying my sense we're being spied on, even though we haven't found any new cameras."

Noah tossed his arms around her, holding her close before he kissed her.

She stayed in his arms, wanting nothing more than for that moment to become their new normal. Hoping the next day and the day after that could end without either of them worrying if a murderer might be watching their every move or planning on making their next kiss their last.

Noah sighed, and Winter stood back from him to look him in the eye.

"What is it? You went all rigid there, and not in a good way."

His lips tightened into a grimace. "They found another body. Kristine Tippett, a twenty-seven-year-old woman. Same M.O. as the Abbott and Wald cases, except now we have a female victim, so our profile is changing."

"So Falkner has you investigating the case now. That's a good thing, right?"

Noah let her go. "Not really. I spent the morning briefing Cyber on what I'd found out about the app, which wasn't much. I mostly answered questions about search terms I'd tried. They're taking over that side of things, which is great for me. But Falkner had me interviewing all afternoon. Eight witnesses from the latest murder."

"Did you get anything?"

"Damn little. It happened in that little art house movie theater, the Marquee. Witnesses all had the same story. The people who worked there said they cleaned the theater, and it was empty. Only one ticket was sold for that showing, and the staffer who sold it identified the victim. She arrived as the film started and headed straight for the bathroom after buying her ticket. She probably found a seat after the opening credits were over."

"And nobody noticed someone being murdered during the film?"

"It was a slasher film about a killer clown who uses amusement park rides to terrorize his victims before stabbing them to death."

"So lots of screaming."

"Yep. And it was an earlier screening. The theater was empty except for the killer and the victim."

"Are you going to the crime scene tomorrow, or is that more work for the twins?"

He sniffed and smiled. "Clones. And, no, it won't be me going out there. Falkner wants me on desk duty for the duration."

Winter clutched his shirt. "That makes no sense. You're the best they've got."

He held her hand against his chest. "Thanks for the vote of confidence, but the rest of the team isn't half bad at what they do."

"So…why not add your skill to theirs? What's Falkner afraid of?"

The answer was clear enough to her, but she needed to hear him say the words, to confirm that the Bureau was even less of a friend to her than it had been when she was an agent.

Her former SSA, one Aiden Parrish, had given Winter reason—on more than one occasion—to believe the private sector would be a better place for her. It seemed Noah's boss felt the same way, and the attitude was making his job that much harder.

"Falkner has a media blackout in place for the Tippett murder because he doesn't want to panic the public. But when it gets out, he's concerned your name will get picked up because Wald was your client."

"I don't want that getting out any more than Falkner does. But it's not out yet, and the public already knows about Terry Abbott and Ernst Wald."

He nodded. "I know, but Falkner's worried anything we do will make this blow up in his face. You know what the press will do if they get wind of us." Noah made quotation marks with his fingers. "'Private eye wife of an agent first on the case, leaving FBI in the dirt.'"

Winter took a step backward, floored by the revelation. "That's crazy. I'm just a private investigator. You're a talented field agent with an incredible record. Maybe Falkner's saving you for where he can use you best? You know how secretive SSAs are. They never tell you what they have in the works. Or have you forgotten how communicative Aiden Parrish could be?"

Noah laughed as he headed for the kitchen. "That man could talk circles around you without saying a word. But at least he'd let you know what he'd been thinking at the end of the day. Falkner…he's a different kind of fish."

She watched Noah pull a bottle of bourbon out from behind a row of reds in a cupboard. "Sometimes, I miss the badge and what it allowed me to do. But I like my freedom. I just wish my professional life and private one weren't at odds so much of the time. Is my job really making your life hell?"

He set the bottle on the kitchen counter. "Of course not. I'm proud of what you've accomplished. What Falkner fears has nothing to do with you. It's me. He and I have never seen eye to eye."

She joined him in the kitchen and opened another cabinet, taking down two old-fashioned glasses. "Give it time. Aiden wasn't the easiest guy to work with back in Richmond, and he eventually warmed up to us." She set the glasses on the counter.

He picked up the bottle and motioned to them. "You don't like bourbon."

She lifted the bottle from his hands and twisted off the cap. "I also don't like to see you drinking alone. Whatever's bothering you bothers me."

Winter poured out two fingers for each of them.

Noah lifted his glass and glanced around the kitchen. "Are you feeling less paranoid now? Did you figure out if we actually do have any more eyes on us?"

Winter peered into her glass. "I swept when I got home. And then again ten minutes after that, when I wasn't satisfied with the first sweep. We're good."

She took a deep sip. The burn in her throat turned to a bitter aftertaste, but the fire the bourbon awakened in her belly chased away the chill her current case had instilled in her.

"Have you learned anything about where those cameras came from? We need to figure that out…and soon…if we're ever going to have a real life."

She rolled the amber liquid around in her glass. "A few router addresses run out of nearby homes and businesses. They're all proxied and piggybacked somehow. Whoever's doing it, they know computers and network technology like the back of their hand. Kinda like whoever created that dating app."

Noah emptied the contents of his glass and set it on the counter. "I want our damn lives back."

She leaned against the counter beside him. "I want the same thing. We've got something special here, and I'm not going to lose it to some psycho, or psychos, plural. Not if I can help it."

"Ditto, Mrs. Black-Dalton. It's us against the world."

Winter smiled, warmed by his words and the bourbon. All she had to do now was hunt down a killer, expose a Peeping Tom who kept recording them, and ensure nothing terrible happened to her or Noah in the process.

25

Winter sat at her desk, mocha by her side and tablet open to Wandering Hearts. She and Noah had spent the rest of Friday evening planning for a sting meeting with whoever had been messaging Terrier's and Grizzly's profiles. Ariel would be in soon to discuss the plan.

The idea forming in Winter's mind was that the killer selected her victims based on criteria like arrogance, a desire to "try something new," and a pathetic proclamation of love for the spouse they wanted to step out on, as if that absolved them of their dirty deeds. Both Terry Abbott and Ernst Wald, fools that they were, had expressed similar sentiments in their ill-fated profiles.

Last night, while reviewing bios with Noah, they speculated that those factors could be triggers for the killer, so Winter updated her fake profiles to match. That way, if their sting target wasn't the actual killer, they'd still have a well-baited hook.

"Can't get what I want at home. Please tell me real sex isn't dead. I'm looking for someone with more than a pulse. I'm not even thirty!"

The statement felt absurd when she read it back to herself, but she could imagine people feeling that way.

If the Wandering Hearts user numbers were any indication, plenty of people did.

She opened Kline's profile and added a new status there as well, toning it down a little to match his age.

"Been too long since I've known a warm touch. I need more than this."

Winter chuckled as she reread the update, imagining grumpy, shuffling Kline "Grizzly Bear" Hurst acting sweet and romantic.

Everybody needed somebody, of course, and age was no barrier to love. At least, it shouldn't have been, though the majority of profiles Winter had seen on the app were people in their mid- to late forties.

Seems the old mid-life crisis statistic is as reliable as ever.

As she closed out the profile, Ariel bounced in from the street. "Hey, Boss. Anything new and exciting on that app?"

"Just the usual requests for role-playing between the sheets. Or, in one case, on the kitchen sink. Come on in, so we can talk sting plans."

Ariel stepped through the door into Winter's office off the main room and rubbed her hands together. "I'm helping catch a killer. That's a bucket list item. Check!"

Winter wagged a finger at her. "You need to think about one particular word you just said. 'Killer.' Keep this quiet… because the cops aren't releasing details yet…but another murder occurred Thursday night."

"One more straying husband bites the dust, huh?"

Winter pitched her pen onto the desk and sat back, staring into Ariel's eyes.

The younger woman's smile faltered, and she humbly settled herself into a chair. "Sorry. I know it's not fun and games."

"The victim was also a woman this time."

That put Ariel on alert. Her head snapped up. "Are we sure it's the same killer? Could it be a copycat? Or maybe it's a husband-and-wife team, taking out cheaters together."

Hearing her assistant spin up profiling ideas reminded Winter of the best times she'd had in the Bureau, working with Autumn and the team in Richmond. Sitting around the conference table throwing ideas into the pot until it simmered into a trail they could follow to stop a killer.

Maybe she has what it takes to do this job after all. She certainly has her head in the game.

Even so, enthusiasm was only one ingredient in the recipe.

"It's great to hear you thinking that way, but if we continue with this plan, you could be in danger. You have to understand, this isn't television. Real people have been real murdered."

Ariel nodded in double time and put a hand on Winter's desk. "I knew the risks when I applied to work here, just like I knew them when I applied to the Police Academy."

Winter picked up her pen. "As your employer, and the more experienced investigator, I'm responsible for your safety. Noah and I will be in the room with you, monitoring everything that goes on. We'll be right there and ready to step in."

Her assistant relaxed in the chair. "I trust you to watch out for me, and I won't do anything stupid. Promise. No thrilling heroics for this girl."

"Good, but I need to be clear. This isn't meant to be like hanging a worm out to catch a fish. We're hoping to get a visual on the person meeting you and to maybe capture some photographs if we can manage it."

"Sounds like the basics of P.I. work, like you always say, right? Sixty percent sitting around, twenty percent playing shutterbug, and twenty percent running errands for overworked legal teams."

Winter laughed and was about to launch into a rundown of how she, Noah, and Ariel would conduct their sting and stakeout at Magro's later that night when her tablet chimed with a notification. She opened the device to see that Wandering Hearts had sent a message to Terrier's profile.

Though Winter wanted to read it alone, Ariel was leaning forward over her desk and had to have noticed the app logo.

"Is that for me?"

"It's for Terrier." Winter tempered her voice to sound firm. "Who is not you, remember?"

Ariel's elation subsided. "I got that part. So what does the message for the nonexistent me say?"

"It's from our suspect. Or an alt profile, I guess. This one's called *unbreakmyheart2*. They're asking if you want to meet for lunch at the Peek-a-Brew café instead."

"I know the place. It's not far from here." Ariel stepped around the desk and hovered over her boss's shoulder. "So what are you waiting for? Accept."

Winter lowered her hands to her lap. "It's not that easy. Noah and I already did a quick survey of Magro's, and you've been there recently. It's familiar territory. This throws all of that out the window."

"Peek-a-Brew is super out in the open. Like, big windows and little bistro tables on the sidewalk outside. The servers also wear the hottest outfits, by the by, not that you're looking. But I am, so there's that."

Her assistant's enthusiasm continued to ramp up as she described the entrance to the café, where the exits and restrooms were located, and how many people were usually there over the lunch hour.

For the second time that morning, Winter felt renewed

appreciation for Ariel's presence and commitment to her business.

"Law enforcement might not be in your future, but you have an investigator's mindset. Remind me not to let you jump ship when something better comes along."

Ariel's eyebrows flew up. "As if. I'm here for the duration, Boss. As long as you'll have me. So we're having lunch at Peek-a-Brew, right?"

"Yes, we are." Winter typed out a reply confirming lunch at a quarter after noon, then sat back and folded her arms. "We need to take precautions. Noah needs to know about the change in location, and despite your exceptional eye for details, he and I still need to recon the place beforehand."

"Sounds like you better get moving."

Winter's jaw slipped open, but her assistant's bubbly attitude had returned. It was hard to stomp on that kind of enthusiasm. "Let's pretend you phrased that as a question. This is me saying, yes, I'd better get moving. I have a husband to pull away from reruns of the *Real Housewives of Dallas*."

"He watches what now? Why did I think he spent his weekends watching bass fishing tournaments?"

"I haven't the slightest clue, but don't put the idea in his head. The last thing I need is for him to get excited about a hobby." Ariel opened her mouth to speak, but Winter was already packing up her tablet. "Plan to be at Peek-a-Brew by noon."

"I need to go change."

Winter examined Ariel, assessing her blouse, knee-length pencil skirt, and booties and concluding they counted as "date-worthy attire."

Her assistant, however, clearly felt differently. "It won't take me more than ten minutes to pick out a new outfit. Promise. There's a server named Anton who I can't believe is still single. At least, he was the last time I checked."

"Ariel, I don't want to squash your plans for romance, but we're preparing to stakeout a possible murder suspect, and it could be someone with more aptitude for killing and evading capture than you seem willing to accept. It's okay to back out."

Ariel paced in the closed space of Winter's office before stepping out to the larger room beyond. She went to her desk, hefted her bag, and turned back around. "I'm just getting into character. Imagining it's a real date so I can give off 'real date' vibes. Besides, you'll be there to protect me. I'm not worried."

26

Noah waited, with coffee in each hand, while Winter unlocked the door to her office. She'd called him down after letting him know about the change in their planned stakeout.

"One mocha for the lady." He handed her the drink and followed her inside.

He and Winter went back to the kitchen, where she explained how their evening meeting at Magro's had been changed to a lunch date at the Peek-a-Brew café.

"We have less than an hour to get there, but I don't want to show up too soon. If the killer is the one who's been messaging me, they're probably conducting their own stakeout."

"So we should walk up separately and act like nothing's expected. I'll go in first and grab a table by the counter. If I spot anyone who sets off alarm bells, I'll text you. If all looks clear, you join me. Ariel will move into position once we're inside."

A knot formed in Noah's stomach as he thought about what they were doing.

He sank against the kitchen counter. "She's taking a huge risk. What if the killer's on to us and is carrying a weapon? Are we going in armed?"

"No. We'll be in a public place, and it's unlikely this killer's going to strike in the middle of the day in a crowded lunchroom. It's not an empty, dark, loud theater with surround sound."

"But the shift in plan means anything's on the table."

"That's true," she nodded, "but this could also be our only chance to get eyes on the killer."

"And you mentioned this to Ariel?"

"Not in so many words, but she's ready to work."

Noah wrapped his arm around her. "So tell me about this café."

She rested her head against his shoulder. "I swung by before I came home. The place matches Ariel's description. It's a small building that seats about twenty-five or so. There're tables around the dining floor and a few along the street side of the building. It's set between two storefronts. A sporting goods shop and one of those twenty-four-hour, fresh-baked cookie places."

"Did you go inside?"

"The only access to the kitchen is through a break in the serving counter, which faces the picture windows along the street. Restrooms are at the back, down a narrow hall that's half-blocked by mop buckets and stacked boxes of paper products."

He scoffed. "Fire department's going to love seeing that when they come through on a safety inspection. What's the entrance look like?"

"One way in to the customer-facing area. Single door, framed in wood. Brick facade. It's an older building. Older than my office."

"Okay. You got a good breakdown." He took a deep breath, expanding his chest. "We should get going. I'll set up at a table to the side of the room, with good sightlines to the entrance and kitchen."

Winter raised her head and met his eyes, studying his face. "Thank you. I feel better knowing you'll be there with me."

Noah chuckled. "This stakeout will be the most excitement I've had since your last case."

She sat up. "What about those traffickers you helped bring down?"

"You mean the ones connected to the case you were working for that Schumaker guy? Darlin', if I'm being honest, I envy you. The Bureau's been great. It's let me do things I've always wanted to. Stopping bad things from happening to good people. It's why I joined the Dallas PD after the Marines."

"But?"

She'd always been able to read him, and there would be no keeping his thoughts to himself now that she'd started probing for the truth.

Noah stood up straight. "I've been reevaluating my position there. Considering what I'll do if things don't change."

She finished her mocha and set the cup on the counter.

When he looked her way, he saw the question burning in her eyes. "Go ahead. Ask away, because I'll never keep a secret from you."

She pushed off the counter and planted a kiss on his mouth. "If the day comes that you want to leave the Bureau, talk to me about it first. We've only been here a few months. I don't want you to give up your dream because of a rough adjustment period."

He wrapped his arms around her waist and held her tight. "You'll be the only person I come to."

"And if you want to be a writer or a pastry chef, I'll support you just like you've always supported me."

Noah's chuckle rolled around in his chest like thunder. "A pastry chef?" He laughed again. "Now there's an idea."

27

Noah removed his jacket and hung the outerwear on the hook beside the booth he'd snagged for him and Winter. She'd arrived within minutes of his text and now sat across the table from him.

They'd left a note with Detective Darnell Davenport about what they were doing. He said he'd alert patrol to monitor the area but couldn't commit more than one unit to the task.

The booth he'd chosen was close to the counter, and Noah had a good view of the front door. Winter sat opposite him, giving her a view of the service counter, deli cases, kitchen, and the hallway to the restrooms. It also hid her face from the majority of onlookers. She had to consider that the killer might recognize her.

It had meant driving through downtown traffic, but they'd arrived in time to avoid the lunch rush. The crowds showed up minutes after he and Winter had placed their orders. Two other couples were already eating. One was a pair of young women, probably in college. They held hands across the table and traded laughs as they ate. The other couple was older, closer to Jack and Beth in age, and quietly nibbled at their salads.

A mother with a young child entered and shuffled to the nearest table inside the door. She had a diaper bag over one shoulder and struggled under the burden as she fought with the tot to keep his hair smoothed down. He giggled and swiped at her hand like he was being attacked by bees.

Their presence could be problematic if their mystery date was, in fact, the killer and decided to strike. Noah made a note to head to the mother and child first if they needed to empty the dining room quickly.

Unless she's the killer. Dammit.

The irony of the thought wasn't lost on him, but he couldn't bring himself to chuckle.

Two women in business suits entered and joined the growing line that now stretched from the counter to the door.

The only other person in the room was Ariel, seated at a table in the center. She faced the picture windows that lined the sidewalk while typing on a laptop, an open book on her lap.

Noah got comfortable in his own seat, staying alert but struggling to keep his eyes off Winter. She'd worn her black hair flowing around her shoulders, which surprised him. She usually wore a ponytail, and often tied it in a back bun during field work. Yet there she was, looking relaxed and casual as ever. She'd even applied a touch of rouge lipstick. The effect took his breath away.

I'm the luckiest dang guy in the world.

She caught his gaze and smiled. "The makeup was Ariel's idea. She said an ex-girlfriend showed her a trick and she wanted me to look like I was meeting my husband for lunch. The hair was mine. Helps keep me undercover."

"You need to give that woman a raise." He glanced around

the dining room. The line was moving quickly, and Peek-a-Brew servers in their figure-hugging uniforms carried plates and trays of food around the room. Not too much flesh was on display, but Noah couldn't argue the employees were intended to be just as much of an attraction as the food, brew, and craft beer.

He went back to monitoring the room, observing casually until a young man in a crop top that showed off his six-pack approached with a tray holding two sodas and their lunch order.

"Roast beef on white and a pastrami Reuben?"

He set down the drinks first, then the plates, and asked if they needed anything else. Noah was distracted by movement at the door, but Winter told him they were fine. The server gave a slight bow before stepping away.

"All good?" Winter picked up her sandwich.

The mother and her child stood in line without the diaper bag.

"Got a possible complication. Mother and child by the door. They're in line now. Diaper bag left behind to hold their table."

Two tours in Iraq had given Noah more than enough reason to worry about anything that could conceivably contain an IED. Piles of trash, cars left parked in odd places...or sometimes right where you'd expect them to be.

And unattended bags.

At the table in the center of the room, Ariel shifted her laptop to make room for a glass of lemonade delivered by a woman wearing Daisy Dukes with a white crop top. The plan was for her to wait until their guest arrived and then order food. That'd give Noah and Winter more time to observe and determine if the mystery person was their killer or a genuine date.

Noah nodded at Winter, then moved to the edge of his

bench seat, thinking of a way he could check the diaper bag without being obvious.

The line moved. The mother and child were near the counter, but she suddenly jerked to the side with a hand over her nose. Scooping her son up, she headed straight back to the table by the door.

Noah casually shifted back to the center of his seat as she grabbed the bag and raced toward the restrooms.

Winter patted his hand. "There's one threat I guess we can write off." Noah checked his watch as she bit into her sandwich and spoke around the food. "How long now?"

Keeping his eyes glued to the door, he lifted his own sandwich. "About ten minutes still. Here's hoping the person's punctual."

The minutes ticked by as Noah kept vigilant surveillance of the entrance.

Their server offered refills of their drinks, and he was pleased to see Ariel getting the same treatment from Daisy Dukes. She looked their way, tilted her glass, and slurped from the straw while glancing around the room.

"This is the last time she's coming on any covert ops."

Winter smirked. "She has a great head for inquiry and investigation. Field work may not be her forte…yet…but she's learning. Even you were a green recruit once. Cut the girl some slack, cowboy."

Noah rechecked his watch. It was twenty after twelve. Their date was late or a no-show.

Winter removed her tablet from her messenger bag. "I'm going to see if our lunch date sent a message."

Noah chewed another bite of his sandwich, his edginess souring his ability to enjoy the food.

Still beats an MRE in the middle of the desert any day.

He would've preferred greater control of the scene and to have the place loaded with his people along with backup on the street outside. But because this was Winter's operation, he had to defer to her.

"Nothing from our mysterious Wandering Hearts user, not from either profile." Winter put her tablet away.

"Why am I not surprised."

Noah kept an eye on the people walking in and out. As time passed, though, he felt certain their Wandering Hearts user wouldn't show. In a way, he was relieved. He and Winter weren't prepared for fireworks if something went wrong.

As he monitored the crowd in his peripheral vision, the mother and her now-wailing little boy whisked through the room, where the young woman struggled to open the door. Noah, thoroughly convinced she was a bomber or murderer by now, jumped up to help.

She gave an abrupt "thanks" before storming her way down the sidewalk, suspicious bag in tow.

"And you want one of those little humans," Winter said as he sat back down.

He glanced at his wife but ignored her comment. "This reminds me of the stakeouts we used to do. It's fun working with you again. I missed that."

She rested her arms on the table, getting comfortable. "You were, and still are, the best partner I ever had."

He held his soda cup in front of his lips. "Do you miss it? Working with the Bureau? Any regrets?"

She tossed her head, her shiny hair catching the light through the window. "Sometimes, but I'm pretty happy being my own boss. Speaking of which, my employee thinks we got stood up. She just texted me."

"You sure?"

"My guess is we've all been playing goldfish in the perpetrator's fishbowl. I'm going to tell her she can go. There's a coffee shop across the street. I noticed a tall blond woman getting up and leaving from an outside table."

"Tall women are always trouble. That's why I married one. To keep an eye on her."

She swatted at him. "Be serious. I saw the woman sitting there when we arrived. And she didn't just finish her latte and leave."

"What do you mean?"

"I mean she *fled* the instant you started heading for the door."

28

Winter kept a sharp eye out the entire walk back to her downtown office. She didn't want to take any chances. Their mystery guest might have no-showed or might have been running her own stakeout.

And if that was her running from the coffee shop, she could still be spying on us from a car around here.

Ariel was probably at her desk already, having driven back from the café. Winter and Noah had briefly flirted with the idea of getting into her assistant's car, but they'd decided to maintain the ruse, just in case the killer had been watching.

Winter made a point of noting each vehicle that passed her on the road as she walked a few feet behind Noah. He shuffled ahead with his head up and his eyes alert for threats.

When they reached the office door awhile later, Kline was pacing the floor with his phone in hand.

Ariel sat at her desk, rolling her eyes at the older man. "Grumpy grizzly texted me and said he wanted to know how things went, so I told him to meet us here."

Kline shuffled over to Ariel's desk and grunted.

"Grumpy's right. She's out risking her neck like a dang fool. Of course I'm gonna get grumpy about it."

Unable to hold in a laugh, Winter shuffled up to him and patted his shoulder. "That's sweet, but I have grandparents for that, Kline. And a husband." She held out a hand as if presenting Noah for inspection, which had the effect of making her assistant snort and Kline get even grumpier.

"Well, are ya gonna keep me in the dark all day? What happened?"

They'd grown closer in the few months he'd been her contractor, repairing and upgrading the office space until it was picture-perfect and to her liking.

But Winter wasn't quite ready for Kline to sound like a father chastising a teenager out after curfew.

Apparently, Noah felt the same way. "Settle down there, wild man."

Ariel added her own biting remark. "Yeah, who made you boss of the boss?"

Kline looked ready to offer a retort of his own, so Winter shut the bickering down with a chop of her hand. "We're fine. Nothing happened."

Kline pocketed his phone with a shaking hand and turned to Winter. "Nothing happened, huh?"

"Nope. Our mystery date was a no-show."

"Possibly," Noah added. "Winter, I'm gonna head home. I'll stop by Jack and Beth's first, just to check in and see how they're doing."

"Give the place another sweep while you're there?"

He smiled. "I'm almost hurt you feel you need to ask, darlin'. Of course I will." With a quick kiss, he made his exit, leaving Winter with her assistant and contractor, both of whom leveled expectant stares at her.

Kline rubbed his hand over his brow. "What's the plan now?"

"The plan is for me to review my mental notes from the failed stakeout." She headed to her office and took a seat at her desk.

Kline stepped into her office and approached her. "You should let me handle the Grizzly Bear profile."

"Why would I do that?"

"You might not come across as a man."

Winter drummed her fingertips on the desk. Maybe Kline had a point.

She held up her index finger. "If I agree, you'll share all messages with me. There'll be no going rogue. No contact with anybody who messages you on the app, and you only use the app from my tablet, in this office."

Kline lifted the left side of his mouth in a half smirk. "You sound like my mother."

"I mean it, Kline. I won't allow any of this unless I can protect you."

He gave her a curt nod. "I understand. I won't do anything stupid, just as long as you assure me the same. People planting cameras around you means we're all vulnerable."

Winter's stomach tightened at the mention of the surveillance, and she melted into her chair.

Kline's voice drew her back from her worry. "So can I take over that account?"

She stared at her contractor, trying to ignore the burning sensation in her gut. "All right. But everything you do goes through me. If you're going to send a message, check with me first. And let's have you active on the app in the morning and late afternoon, so it looks like you're scrolling outside the workday."

She continued detailing the protections she wanted in place to ensure his safety, including no use of the app at his apartment.

"It's possible the person we're dealing with is masking their IP address, which means they might be able to uncover other people's."

"Fair enough. No at-home dallying. Sign out before I leave your office."

Ariel poked her head in, suggesting a few profiles she'd found on the app that appeared promising. "They're all in their early- to mid-forties, which isn't saying much, I guess. And they don't have profile photos, either, so they could be playing coy or being secretive. But get this, two of them mention the Black Cat Motel."

That was the lead Winter had been hoping for. Something concrete to connect a profile on the app to one of their crime scenes. While not necessarily a firm lead—or even a good one—it gave her a thread to tug just the same.

29

The outskirts of Austin featured an assortment of cheap motels and coffee shops cluttering a strip on the I-35 corridor. A sign ahead with a black cat standing on all fours with its tail raised and teeth bared wasn't the welcome Winter expected from a motel associated with secret trysts.

The two-story, L-shaped, black building that faced the highway seemed more appropriate for a Halloween funhouse. The windows appeared blacked out, and someone had painted the parking lot and pool in front black too. Atop the black roof, two yellow cat eyes peered out onto the highway.

This is gonna be fun.

Why Terry Abbott had arrived at this motel, as opposed to one more fitting of a man of his means, was less of a mystery now that Winter had become versed in the Wandering Hearts userbase. Since building the fake profiles for Kline and Ariel, she'd scrolled through users with backgrounds in finance and politics, as well as users who worked in the trades and even a few who had just finished college.

It seemed the app catered to the tastes of just about anybody with an urge they didn't want to bother trying to control for a more vanilla partner.

She parked next to the office where stickers of black cats covered the glass windows out front. A blast of hot air hit her face when she walked inside.

The small office featured posters of the Austin high-rise, gumball machines, and a few racks of dusty maps. A wooden check-in desk touted pamphlets of tourist sites. Hooks covered the wall behind that, displaying two sets of keys for each room. Considering their clientele, updating to electronic keys might've been safer and more cost-efficient.

A man stepped out from a doorway behind the counter. Craggy, with a sparse gray beard and beady brown eyes, he walked with a slight limp as he approached the counter. He had a barrel chest, and Winter could smell the stench of cigarette smoke on his clothes from across the room.

"Well, hey there, missy. You want a room?" His smile showed off the gap in his front teeth.

Winter eased closer to the desk. "I'm looking for information about the man who died here a few days ago. Terry Abbott."

The manager gave her a surly grin. "You a cop?"

"Private detective." She removed a card from her jacket pocket. "I'm Winter Black from Black Investigations."

He took the card and glanced at her information. "Everybody calls me Gus."

She appraised the lobby. "Hell of a place you got here, Gus."

He set the card on the counter. "It's good for travelers and folks who need a place to stay for a night."

"Do you get a lot of repeat customers?" Winter leaned against the counter. "Maybe somebody showing up with a different date every time?"

Gus chuckled. "I get a lot of regulars, sure. It's always married people wanting to cheat. I can usually spot 'em a mile away. The nervous ones looking over their shoulder are always married."

Winter ran her fingers across a dusty pamphlet. "Anybody in particular stand out as more regular than the rest?"

Gus's smile faded. "I don't know what you're getting at, but I can tell ya I don't care for being interrogated under my own roof. And since you ain't a cop, I guess this's the only roof you and I'll ever be chatting under."

"Fair enough, Gus, and I'll do my best to respect your... roof. I'm just trying to track down a murderer who may be using your business premises to scout for and, at least in Terry Abbott's case, kill their targets. Do you remember who he came with?"

Gus shook his head. "I didn't remember who had the room until I saw the dead guy on the floor. I'll never forget the expression on his face, I tell ya."

"Could it have been a man or a woman?" Winter's hopes began to dim. "Anything you can remember would be a great help."

Gus tugged at the wispy curls atop his head. "Sorry. I told the police I never saw who went into the room with him. I can't say if he was into men or women. We get a lot of both around here."

Winter studied the keys on the wall, where each room number had two keys available. "Were two sets of keys taken for that room?"

Gus dropped his hand from his hair and nodded. "I had two checked out for that room. Both were inside with the dead guy."

"And he checked them both out?"

The motel manager ran a hand over his chin. "You know,

for not being a cop, you sure sound like one. Pretty much the exact same questions as that detective asked me."

"I have a background in law enforcement, so that's not surprising."

"Sounds like I'm being interrogated after all."

She gave him a pretty smile. "I prefer to think of this as an interview, Gus. Not an interrogation. Would you be okay if I asked a few more questions?"

"Aw, heck. Go ahead. I'll tell you everything I told the cops and those FBI guys who came around. Couple of chuckleheads if I ever saw 'em, but they were polite enough."

Winter figured he was referring to the Weston Clones. She'd have to tell Noah later.

"Okay, Gus…and please tell me if I'm not being polite… my previous question. Did Terry Abbott check out both keys to his room the night he was murdered?"

The motel manager *mm-hmm*ed.

"Do you have record of him making the reservation?"

"Sure don't. All my transactions are in cash, and I ain't too stringent when it comes to checking IDs. That's why people come here. They know I don't care about details. Just as long as they leave the room as they found it, I don't say nothin'."

"What if a repeat offender leaves a messy or damaged room? How do you charge them if you don't keep records or use credit cards?"

Gus rested his elbow on the counter. "Have you seen my rooms? It ain't the Hilton. Alls I do is change the towels and sheets. I rarely replace anything that gets damaged. No one coming here seems to notice."

Winter let out a long sigh of frustration. "What about a register? Got one of those?"

"The police already checked my register and took it as evidence. Said I'll get it back, but that I should probably have another one in the meantime."

"Do you remember if Terry Abbott signed in that night?"

Gus chuckled, sounding like a fish on land gasping for air. "I had four John Does signed in that night and two Jane Smiths. Like I told you, no one coming here wants their identity known."

Winter's suspicion the killer had used the establishment before began to take hold. They must've known about Gus's lackadaisical check-in policy. She glanced at the wall behind the desk, where a small camera pointed down at her. "Do you still have the footage from your camera?"

Gus followed her gaze. "That thing hasn't worked in years. Broke six months after I got it put in. Never bothered to get it fixed. Waste of money."

Winter shrank against the counter. She'd hit another dead end. She was thankful most motel owners were more responsible than the disheveled manager of the Black Cat. Men like Gus made investigative work a nightmare.

"I'm sure your dead man was here having an affair. No other reason to come here. Things got out of hand, and someone killed him." Gus shrugged, showing off a disinterested smirk. "This ain't the first place that's happened, and it won't be the last. Problem is, ever since the murder, my business has been down. Sure hope they catch 'em so I can start making money again."

His disregard for a man who'd died at his place of business rattled Winter.

She gestured to the card still on the counter. "If you think of anything, call me day or night."

So much for a lead coming from all those profiles mentioning this place. Unless old Gus is involved. But the only thing I can see him killing is a pack of unfiltered cigarettes.

With more frustration building, Winter headed back to her office, then detoured and aimed herself back home instead.

A week spent tracking a killer with a taste for up-close and personal murder had Winter almost ready to start building barricades around their property. She needed to wrap this case up so she could stop looking in two directions at once.

As soon as she busted this dating-app killer, she and Noah could hunker down and catch their mysterious spy.

In the meantime, though, the killer might still be out there adding notches on their belt. Winter would go home… but not to build a wall to hide behind. She and Noah would put their heads together and figure out their next step, just like they'd always done.

30

Miranda Freeman checked her hair and makeup in the brass plaque placed outside the door of the Firebomb Nightclub. The trendy bar and dance spot had been a hit with the city's up-and-comers. She'd never dared to go there in the past, but when user *unbreakmyheart2* told her he could get them on the upper dance balcony, her excitement overflowed.

Sid had gone off to some plumber's convention for the next few days, so the timing for her meeting couldn't have been better. Her bed remained littered with the fancy cocktail dresses she'd taken home from the boutique where she worked. She'd spent hours applying and reapplying her makeup.

As she stepped inside thick brass and wood doors, the beat of the music vibrated through the walls. A podium waited just inside the entrance.

There, a man in a tuxedo greeted her with a wary eye. "Name?" His tone came out snooty.

She froze, unsure of what name to use. She decided to keep it simple. "Ah, Miranda."

He offered a curt nod and walked over to a red velvet

rope to the right that cordoned off a flight of dimly lit steps. "Your party is waiting for you on the mezzanine."

Miranda wanted to squeal with excitement. She'd dreamed of such treatment when she met Sid. He'd wined and dined her, showing her an extravagant lifestyle. Once they'd exchanged vows, however, the high life disappeared. He became an old man in her eyes, never wanting to go out or attend fancy parties. And she became a repressed housewife.

Things changed between them after that.

They had fights over her taking a job at the boutique, but he eventually gave into her wishes. Miranda didn't care. If she couldn't participate in the glittery affluence she'd hoped Sid would provide, she'd find another way in. After all, Miranda always got whatever she went after.

Giddy, she climbed the dark wooden steps to the next level. All her life, she'd strived to be better than the other girls in Wichita Falls. She'd run faster in track and bedded more boys than all the rest. She'd learned a lot about men before finishing high school and had planned on using those skills to catch a rich husband.

While she'd succeeded in that regard, she hadn't obtained a husband with the bedroom skills to truly satisfy her.

Miranda reached the second floor. The music was louder here. When she placed her hand on the walls, the bass vibrated through her fingertips.

She hurried along the corridor where polished wooden panels glistened in the light from the flickering sconces, searching faces to see if anyone recognized her. But no one made eye contact.

The shadows were against her when it came to seeing anyone's face, but that didn't deter her. She eased along, staying in the light, hoping whoever had summoned her would discern her from her app photo.

Ahead, an arched doorway featured a myriad of bobbing floodlights in hypnotizing colors. She sashayed closer, the thump of the music vibrating up her legs. The sexual energy charging through her was like nothing she'd known.

Miranda stepped inside a room with a balcony on the left, stopping at the doorway to adjust her tight dress. The blast of the music sent tingles across her scalp. More music wafted up from below.

She took her time crossing the floor to the balcony, the low lighting impairing her visibility. When she peered over a brass railing at the floor below, an enormous crowd of sweaty, gyrating people packed the dance floor. The entire room throbbed to the pulse-bounding, techno-pop beat. She yearned to be out there, lost in the blissfully happy mass of dancers. A cool breeze swept over her back, and she twisted around to discover the source.

A couple in a tight embrace swayed into a spotlight behind her before sweeping into the dark shadows again. Others spun around the smaller dance floor in the private area, weaving in and out of snippets of light. She discovered dozens of couples in various stages of undress, grinding their hips together in time with the music, moving effortlessly about the half-lit dance floor.

Her cheeks flushed. *Sid would never come to this place.*

Her empty life had driven her to sign on to the Wandering Hearts app, to blot out the pain of her miserable marriage in the arms of another. She deserved one night of happiness before she crawled back into bed with an old man who no longer seemed to love her.

Across the room, a bar sporting a lavender glow from the lights beneath beckoned. A drink. That was what she needed to relax. After, she would hunt for her date.

She made her way through the crowd on the dance floor —tiled to resemble a chess board—taking care to not bump into anyone. Her eyes darted around as she continued searching for the one who'd arranged their meeting, but everywhere she looked, shadows greeted her.

How am I supposed to find anyone in here?

A few feet from the bar, her hopes began to crumble. Maybe he hadn't come because of something she'd said. Or maybe he'd been here, seen her, and left because of her appearance. Miranda was always second-guessing herself.

The patrons gathered at the bar watched the dancers. No couples hovered here, only individual men and women, all taking a break from dancing or scanning the crowds for their next partner. Miranda's enthusiasm returned. She couldn't make out the faces too well, but she was willing to wait and see if her prince charming noticed her.

At the end of the bar, someone stepped out of the shadows and motioned for her to join them. They possessed a come-hither smile.

But that's a woman. I'm meeting a man.

Miranda couldn't make out a single feature in the club's constantly shifting lights. The stranger approached her like a giant cat closing in on its prey.

"You came."

The woman's smooth, silky voice—like a fine wine hitting the edge of a crystal goblet—was like no other. And entirely unlike anything Miranda was expecting from her date.

She put out her hand as if to push the woman back a step. "Hi, I'm here to meet someone. A man named Alex."

A gloved hand rested two fingers against her lips.

"I know who you are. Alex sent me to collect you. I'm his...finder." The woman, dressed in a sleek black dress, took her hand.

"His finder? Like, an assistant?"

The woman covered her mouth with her gloved hand as

she giggled. "Yes, something like that. I'll take you to him now. Come with me."

Miranda's mind raced with doubt, but her body urged her to give in to whatever was happening. She needed this. She'd dreamed about it since her wedding night.

The woman led her back into the corridor, continuing to lay gentle touches on Miranda's arms and around her jawline. She traced the outline of her lips with the tip of a gloved finger.

The sensation sent a jolt of electricity through Miranda's belly. All doubts fell away and she laughed, anxious for the coming event while simultaneously wishing the anticipation would never end.

"I'm taking you to a place where you and Alex can be alone," the woman whispered in her ear.

Miranda was putty in the assistant's hands. Once she met Alex, she would submit to whatever he wanted to do to her.

Her escort stopped at a door with a brass plaque that read *Private*.

What was this? A secret room or a game room like in *Fifty Shades of Grey*. *God, let it be that.*

The door swung open, but Miranda couldn't see anything at first.

As her eyes adjusted, a desk along the back wall appeared, along with a filing cabinet and, in the corner, what looked like a safe.

But no Alex. No man waiting with his collar open.

"Where is he?"

Miranda turned halfway around and was pushed backward into the room. She cried out, catching herself against the desk as the woman entered the room and closed the door behind her.

Stepping forward, Miranda attempted to move around

the woman, but an upthrust arm blocked her. She swatted the limb away. "What the hell is this? Where's Alex?"

"He'll be here in a moment. He wants you on the desk, Miranda. I'm to get you ready."

Shaking her head fiercely, Miranda tried to get around the woman again. "No way. I'm not into that. I don't care who he thinks he is. I don't do girl on girl."

"Oh, silly," the woman laughed, "I'm not going to get you ready that way."

Her other arm came up then, and Miranda had just enough time to notice a glint of metal reflecting in the slim band of light that crept around the edges of the door.

A sharp, feral shriek escaped her mouth as a sudden, horrific pain exploded in her chest.

The woman clamped a hand over her mouth and thrust her other hand up again, forcing the agony deeper into Miranda's body. A hot, angry torment flooded through her, pushing and stressing inside her chest, spreading through her arms and into her belly.

Miranda slumped against the desk, scrabbling to find purchase, to prevent herself from sinking to the floor. Weakly, she batted at the woman's face, then tried to grab her hand and pull it away from her chest.

The pain, thick and hot, raced up her throat like burning oil being poured through her veins.

She whipped her head to the side, and the woman's gloved hand slipped away enough for her to cry out. "What's happening?"

Her attacker covered her mouth again. "Now, now. All will be well, Miranda. Your husband will feel sorrow, but he'll be saved from the pain of knowing how little you valued him. Love is so much more than sex, so much more than excitement. Love is forever. And so is death."

The pain worsened, swelling and rippling out to

Miranda's fingertips. She shook, barely able to hold herself or keep from sliding down the desk to her killer's feet.

Because Miranda knew that was who she had met here. The woman in front of her was not her date's assistant. She was the murderer everyone had been talking about, and Miranda had become her newest victim.

Her heart drummed in her ears, louder than the pounding bass from the club outside.

A gush of warmth ran down the side of her dress. Not the pretty one she took so long to choose. She couldn't get any stains on it. She had to return the outfit to the store in the morning.

When catching her breath became more difficult, Miranda panicked. She wanted to push the hand away from her mouth so she could breathe, but her strength had left her.

She crumbled, and her face hit the cold tile. She couldn't figure out why she was down there, her cheek pressing painfully into the floor, but she couldn't move or right herself. Her slowing heartbeat, no longer keeping time with the music, spurred more panic inside her head.

A numbing discomfort climbed her legs. Black dots danced around the faint light trickling into the room. Confusion and pain riddled her burning muscles, and the liquid fire in her chest traveled up her throat and into her mouth.

In that moment, she wished Sid were with her. Why had she taken this risk?

Fear swept over her like a frozen blanket on a frigid night. She could no longer feel her limbs, and the numbness had climbed to her chest. Agony came with every breath, but the pain eased some when she stopped her desperate wheezing for air.

She drifted, floating in and out of consciousness. She

summoned every ounce of strength she had left to call for help, but her lips never moved.

The dark dots expanded into a curtain of black. The last thing she could make out before her vision faded was light on the tile floor beside her face, and her killer's hand placing a small, glinting object on her forehead.

When had everything gone so horribly wrong? *Am I dying?*

Miranda's fears dimmed, and the cold encompassing her body retreated, making way for a lovely warmth that spread from her chest to every part of her body, and she knew she would be okay.

This is better. I'm gonna be fine.

31

A bitter chill lingered in the air as Winter arrived with Noah outside the Firebomb Nightclub in downtown Austin. Darnell had called just as she and Noah finished breakfast to ask her to join him at the two-story building for "a little chat" about the murders.

The outer brick boasted a fiery collage of rising, painted flames while the club's wood and glass doors stood open, allowing several police officers to clutter the entrance. The neon sign above the door was out, but she could easily read the club's name in the bulbs.

Winter stuck close to Noah's side as he flashed his badge to the cops by the door and they slipped into the club. The second they stopped at the podium, the aroma of bleach, stale beer, and cheap perfume accosted her nose.

Eve waited on a set of stairs to the side of the podium. When she saw Winter, her eyes widened, and she fixed Noah with a glare. "Are you crazy? If Weston sees her, he'll go ballistic."

Winter moved forward, prepared to defend herself, but Noah cut her off. "Winter knows as much about this case as I do. She's a valuable asset and is here in a consulting capacity at Austin PD's request."

Sighing, Eve motioned for Noah to follow her up the steps, leaving Winter on the first floor amid the cops and techs.

She felt useless just standing there while the police moved about the crime scene. She wanted to get a look at the victim. Maybe she'd seen them before or had spoken with them on the app. She'd gotten to know a lot of people on there. If she could recognize the face, she could speed up the investigation and link the victim to Wandering Hearts.

Determined to be of some use, she headed up on her own.

Winter spotted the landing on the second floor as the overhead lights chased away the shadows on the stairs. She was lifting a foot to keep climbing when Darnell Davenport rounded the stairwell corner.

"You again?" His grimace morphed into a grin before she could fire back with her own snarky comment, but she gave him a little of his own medicine all the same.

"I thought I was here at your request. Or was the invitation just so you'd be spared the time of coming to arrest me at my home?"

"Black, you and I need to sit down someday and compare notes. I think you're in my pocket, but I'm willing to be proven wrong. Meanwhile, come tell me what you've learned as it relates to my case."

Darnell crooked his finger at her and pivoted into the hallway where he flagged down a uniformed officer. "I want this witness's assessment of the crime. She has inside information that might help us."

Winter followed him, admiring the second floor's pretty woodwork as they made their way to an arched door where several other officers, including Noah and Eve, had gathered.

She caught her husband's defeated look when she spun

around, staying right on Darnell's heels as he entered an open door.

Inside, the overhead lights emitted an offensive glare, and the odor of death assaulted her. After the time spent in the dimly lit hallway, Winter had to let her eyes adjust. It didn't take long to spot the blood on the office floor. The thick, black, coagulated goo stood out from the gray tile.

Her gaze tracked a trail that led back to the side of a desk. The rigid figure in the shimmering cocktail dress didn't appear human.

Winter moved closer. "How long since the murder?"

"Coroner thinks between six and ten hours ago." Darnell stayed by her side as she approached the victim's feet. "Her rigor is almost set, so we're in there somewhere."

Winter knelt and studied the blood-soaked dress. "Where was she stabbed? Heart again?"

Darnell stooped on the floor next to her. "Yep. Same angle of approach. Down and low, driving up into the organ between the fourth and fifth ribs. No word on if we're looking at the same weapon as the others, but M.O. checks out. Coroner'll compare against wound sites on the other victims."

"He hasn't already done that with the first three victims?"

"Oh, he's done it, but hasn't been able to confirm if we're looking at the same weapon or just the same type. Best estimate is an approximately five-inch straightedge blade."

Winter tilted to the side to get a look at the victim. The blood pooled along her cheek detracted from her almost sculpted features. In life, the woman had been beautiful. Striking in a way that reminded Winter of a movie star or supermodel.

"Four victims all stabbed in the same manner isn't luck. That took planning. This crime screams anger to me.

Someone's out for vengeance." Winter eased over to examine the chest wound. "You have a name?"

Darnell got to his feet and opened his phone. "Miranda Freeman. She's married to a local sewer guy named Sid Dwyer. He did my aunt's septic system last year."

Winter spotted the tear in the bodice of the dress. Right between the fourth and fifth rib. The accuracy of the strike meant the killer had the time and ability to aim their knife. Miranda probably didn't see it coming.

"She didn't take her husband's name?" Winter stood, sick of the stench of death.

"You didn't."

"I go by Black-Dalton, when it matters."

Darnell motioned his phone toward the body. "The husband was out of town at a trade convention when we notified him. He was supposed to arrive home this evening. Miranda never mentioned anything to him about going out to a club."

Winter scoured the office for any other clues. "So someone met her at the club, got her trust, brought her in here for a rendezvous, and then killed her. Was there a heart charm again?"

Darnell nodded. "But other than that, nothing. No prints in here except the staff. We're sweeping for DNA, but don't expect to find any. The other murder scenes were clean as well."

"Could the killer have been wearing gloves?"

Darnell put his phone back in his jacket pocket. "That's what I'm thinking." He waved the coroner's team into the room. "You can take over."

Winter backed out of the way, watching as the team in white Tyvek suits placed their toolboxes on the floor not far from Miranda's corpse. She wanted to observe what they collected from the body, an old habit she'd picked up during her days in the Bureau. Overseeing the coroner's team could unearth extra tidbits of information regarding the death.

Instead, Darnell took her elbow and guided her out of the small office. "We're luckier here than at the other places the killer struck." He pointed to a camera in the ceiling molding. "The entire place is covered, and they were all recording."

Winter eyed the lens of the wireless CCTV camera. Easy to install, and with a discreet and tidy appearance, the device offered images available for viewing anywhere, along with secure storage. "Is everything on a drive or uploaded to a server?"

"Both. We'll be watching video for days, but at least we have something. I'm hoping we have the killer leaving the scene."

"Keep me posted on what you find."

"I most definitely will not be doing that." He shook a finger at her. "Here's where we part company, Black, and your involvement ends. If you want updates, check with your husband. It's the FBI's case now as far as I'm concerned."

Out in the hall, Winter spotted Noah and his partner giving SSA Falkner a rundown on the crime scene. Not wanting to cause any more trouble for her husband with his boss, Winter hurried to the stairs.

She swore she heard Darnell snort as she made her quick exit. He probably enjoyed witnessing her speedy escape.

Only when her feet hit the first floor did she allow herself to relax. Seeing no sign of any Bureau personnel nearby, she made a beeline for the door and walked out of the club and into the fresh air.

Winter breathed in and out, clearing the ugly odor of death from her nose as she walked back to Noah's beloved red truck, Beulah.

The nippy morning temperature had her seeking refuge, and she was glad he'd given her the keys. She watched the arrival of more police and FBI agents as she got comfortable and opened her tablet.

After logging into Grizzly Bear's profile, she searched for female users with an age and description that roughly matched the latest murder victim.

Hair color, height, age somewhere in the thirties. White. Slender figure.

Over thirty searches popped up. Finding the victim's profile would take time she didn't have. She was just about to close the app when she saw that two messages had been sent to Grizzly Bear an hour earlier.

One came from a new user named *Morningstar* whose profile contained no information. Unfortunately, Kline had seen the message before Winter and had replied.

Shit. He's using his damn phone.

When she attempted to open the conversation, she received an error message.

We're so sorry, but it seems your message is missing. It was probably deleted because the sender changed their mind.

A tickle of concern rose in Winter's throat. She texted Kline.

Stay off the app when you're not in the office. It's too dangerous. I'll handle all the correspondence from now on.

She waited for a reply he never sent. That wasn't unusual. Sometimes, he'd take all day to text her back. She wasn't sure if it was because he hated cell phones or just wanted to irritate her.

Winter logged out of the app and put her tablet away, unable to shake the blossoming uneasiness in her gut.

Something felt off, but she was damned if she could figure out what.

32

As Winter entered the front door of her office, she wished she'd stopped for coffee. Ariel greeted her by handing her a folded note.

Winter took the paper. "What's this?"

Ariel grinned. "From the old man. He slipped the message under the door before I got here. Apparently, he went to meet someone for breakfast and will be in later."

Unfolding the page to read the words, Winter could barely make out her contractor's chicken scrawl. "Who's he going to meet? Kline doesn't have any friends or family here."

Ariel shrugged and fell into step next to Winter as she hurried to her office. "Maybe he's meeting a new client. About time he finished up with our kitchen."

Winter walked through the glass door. "I like having him around, so stop pushing him away. He's become part of our team."

Ariel sat on the edge of the desk as Winter put her messenger bag in a drawer. "Aw, you like the old geezer. That's sweet."

"Stop calling him that. Kline's done a lot for this business and for me. He's been helping my gramma fix up her house while she recovers too."

Ariel tossed her long, bouncy brown hair around her shoulder. "He told me. He likes your family. And if you want my opinion, he also likes you."

"Don't you have emails to check or messages to answer?"

Ariel jumped from the desk and saluted Winter. "Yes, ma'am. I'm on it."

Winter waited until her assistant walked out of her office before picking up her phone and calling Kline.

In all the time she'd spent with the man at her business, he'd never once left her a note. If he had something to do, he always told her in person. Maybe Miranda's murder had made her paranoid, but she worried about the safety of the two people she'd put on the app.

When Kline didn't answer, she sent him a text.

Got your note. When will you be back in?

Her phone pinged with an incoming text.

With a friend who's in trouble. I'll be in tomorrow.

Winter had to reread the text twice to make sense of it. "I thought he didn't have any friends."

Sitting back in her chair, she stared at his words, stumped. She didn't know a lot about the man. He'd kept most of his life a secret from her. So why should she be surprised if he *did* have a friend in trouble? He probably had neighbors or old acquaintances he kept in touch with.

She slapped her phone screen down on the desk. *Stop this.*

Ariel rushed into her office, her mouth pulled into a taut grimace. "Oh, my god. Oh, my god. You gotta come quick."

Winter scrambled out of her chair. "What is it?"

Ariel pointed back at her desk. "I was opening a few emails, and then my computer went all wonky and stuff. Like it had a glitch." She shook out her hands. "So I did what all the IT guys tell you to do and ran a scan. Well, the scan picked up some kind of surveillance software."

Winter stepped around her desk. "What software?"

Ariel glanced back at her computer. "That's just it. I tried running a trace on it like you showed me with the program we have, but the scan says nothing's there."

Winter's stomach shrank. First the cameras., Now the computers.

Whoever was behind this wanted to know about every aspect of her life and business.

After following Ariel over to her desk, Winter hovered over her assistant's shoulder as she brought up the Task Manager to check out the current programs drawing processing power. "How long would it take you to find out what it is?"

"Me?" Ariel's eyes widened. "I'm not a tech geek. We'd need someone who specializes in spyware or weird software shit for this. Shouldn't we call the police? Someone's been spying on us."

Winter returned to her office and closed her laptop, doing her best to maintain a calm demeanor for the sake of her assistant.

"No need to call the police. The most they might do is file a report we can give to our insurance company if this costs too much to remove from our system. Otherwise, this is out of their league. Shut down your computer." She waved Ariel out of her office. "Let's keep everything to our personal cell phones and the office phones for now. I'll find out who's behind this."

"What if they've tapped into the phones as well?"

The fear quivering Ariel's voice reminded Winter the young woman hadn't signed up to live in a constant state of anxiety. She'd never worked in law enforcement, and no matter how much she might've loved her police dramas on

TV, Ariel didn't understand the emotional toll being on the right side of the law could take.

Her assistant also hadn't lived under the constant dread of what a serial killing little brother might do next. Probably, Winter realized, she herself had become more hardened to this kind of life than most.

She walked out to Ariel's desk and gave her assistant a reassuring squeeze on the arm. "It's just a competitor messing with us. Trying to steal our clients. Happens all the time in this business. Sooner or later, I knew they'd come gunning for me. It's a good sign. It means we've become big competition."

Ariel's shoulders relaxed, and her warm smile returned. "Yeah, you're right."

After returning to her office, Winter dropped the mini blinds and casually closed the door. As it clicked shut, her head began to pound fiercely, forcing her to lean on one of the client chairs for support. The room dimmed around her, and the tension in her head became unbearable as she staggered around her desk.

Dammit. Let me get to the chair. Please let me get to the chair before...

She only just managed to reach the other side before the pressure behind her eyes overpowered her. As had happened multiple times since she suffered a head injury at the hands of The Preacher, Winter dropped to her knees, falling forward across her chair while darkness consumed her vision.

The blackness pulled away gradually, giving Winter a slim line of sight. That sliver of visibility grew to show her the interior of an apartment. She didn't recognize the room or any of the furniture, but she was certain the place didn't belong to anyone she knew. She could only see a simple bed, a nightstand, and a door leading into a darkened bathroom.

None of the items were in good condition, and the few articles of clothing scattered on the bed looked old enough to have belonged to her grandparents during their youth.

Winter turned in a slow circle until she faced the wall that had been at her back. What she saw froze the breath in her chest.

Scenes of her childhood played out as though happening in real time on a movie screen. She and Justin were running around a yard, pushing each other on a tire swing.

This had all happened in the weeks before Douglas Kilroy, The Preacher, had slaughtered Winter's parents, kidnapped Justin, and left her for dead.

The scenes continued to scroll across the wall, moving chronologically through her life to eventually include images from her adult years.

Working with Autumn Trent and the other agents at the Richmond Bureau offices.

Meeting Noah.

Marrying him and moving to Texas. Setting up their home.

These images spoke to her, telling her someone had been observing her all along. Spying on her.

Slowly, painfully, Winter stepped toward the wall, trying to focus—to see anything that might tell her who'd been spying. Who cared to know this much about her?

The vision faded just as Winter glimpsed a picture of her smiling mother, standing outside a small house she didn't recognize. She attempted to hold on, to keep the image in front of her, but everything vanished, turning to wisps of light that melted away, bringing Winter back to her office, back to reality.

No, not yet...

She wanted to scream, but the words caught in her throat.

Winter startled from her vision, the stupor dissipating and leaving her feeling empty and more confused and frightened than she had in a long time. On shaky legs, she rotated her desk chair and hoisted herself into the seat.

Once she was fully settled at her desk, Winter called Noah.

"You okay?" His deep voice soothed her dread.

Winter glanced at her closed laptop, the images of her vision flashing in front of her eyes like memories she could barely hold onto. "I'm at my office. I'm...I've been better. Ariel just discovered we have undetectable spyware on our computers. The security software says the malware's there, but the computer doesn't read it."

"Shit." Noah's anger vibrated through the phone's speaker. "What about cameras? You find any more of those?"

"No, and I've been doing regular sweeps."

"We'll do another one of the house tonight, and we'll check the home computer for spyware too." He sighed. "I don't like this. This is more than someone out to shut down your business or a disgruntled client. Cameras in our home and software that's undetectable...this is a professional. Makes me wonder if your brother has someone hunting you down, or if someone else from one of your past cases with the Bureau is out for you."

The thought of Justin sneaking his way back into her life terrified Winter, and after the vision she'd just had, the very prospect was almost enough for her to suggest protective custody, just to know they wouldn't be under such constant threat. After everything he'd put her through...she'd endured enough torment. She couldn't face that again.

"You really think Justin's back?"

Noah gentled his voice. "He's locked away and will never get out. I promise you, he can't hurt you. I won't let him. We'll get to the bottom of this."

Before Noah hung up, he offered her assurance that everything would be all right, but the words didn't inspire confidence. In her heart, she'd always figured the cameras had something to do with someone keeping an eye on her, and she could imagine her brother doing that.

She sat back, wondering who else in her family might've helped him. Was there anyone Justin could've contacted to uncover Winter's whereabouts? Someone hell-bent on vengeance over his incarceration?

She'd made a fresh start and a new life for herself and her family in Austin. She couldn't ask her grandparents to pack up again and follow her to heaven knew where. Noah had his job, and she had her business.

I'm not running.

No matter what lay ahead, Winter vowed to fight back. Her brother and his sick fan club be damned. If she had to put a bullet in one of Justin Black's devotees, she would. She'd been to hell and back because of him. Enough was enough.

But...what if this is the Wandering Hearts killer?

"Am I missing something here?"

That the killer could be watching her put everything in a new perspective. If they knew about her, they might know about Ariel and Kline too. With that thought in mind, the contractor's text had her even more worried.

Kline doesn't have friends. Ever since he showed up, he's made that clear. He's a loner.

And that meant she couldn't ignore his text. The message might have been a very intentional cry for aid.

I pray I'm wrong because if I'm not, things just got a whole lot worse.

33

Winter stood in the living room holding a mirror up to her ceiling fan, carefully checking each of the lily-shaped sconces to see if any held a camera. She heard Noah rattling around in the kitchen as he pulled out drawers, opened cabinet doors, and rummaged through their pantry, verifying their house was clean.

She hated feeling as if she couldn't relax in her home, but that came with being the sister of a sadistic serial killer. The current case had left her on edge, and this new complication just made everything worse.

Who the hell could be watching her? The Wandering Hearts killer had some tech savvy, but any of Justin's devoted followers could have some know-how too.

Winter doubted she'd ever feel secure again.

"Okay. The kitchen's good." Noah walked into the living room. "I checked the front porch on the way in."

Winter lowered the mirror she'd taped onto the end of a broom handle. "I told Ariel this was a competitor."

Noah chuckled. "I doubt another private detective agency would go to so much trouble. They wouldn't risk getting caught, having their reputation ruined, and possibly losing their license. From what I've seen of Austin, there's plenty of business for everyone."

Winter's phone rang. She reached into the back pocket of her jeans and checked the screen.

When she saw her gramma's name, her heartbeat sped up. "What is it? Are you okay?"

"I'm fine, sweetie. Stop having a fit when I call." Even through the speaker, her grandmother's voice sounded strong. "I was calling to see what happened to Kline."

Winter glanced at Noah. "Kline? Why?"

"He was supposed to start my bathroom rails. Do you have any idea when he's coming by?"

Winter summoned her inner calm. Her first priority was her grandmother's health, and she didn't need to add undue worry to her shoulders. The doctors had warned Winter to make Gramma Beth's life as easy as possible. Any stress could worsen her condition.

"He had to help a friend with an emergency today. He texted me this morning to say he'd be back at work tomorrow. I'll talk to him about rescheduling with you then."

Noah raised his brows, keeping his voice to a whisper with her still on the phone. "Kline has a friend?"

Winter put her finger to her lips, begging him to keep quiet.

"Well, that's fine." Gramma Beth didn't sound bothered by the change in plans. "I do have another question, though. What did you do with those baby pictures you took?"

Winter stared at her cell phone, wondering if her grandmother was indeed feeling well. "What are you talking about?"

"The pictures of you that I keep in the closet. The ones of when you were a little girl. Around four or so, I think. I had them in a box in the bottom of my bedroom closet. I found the box open and a few of your pictures missing. Did you take them?"

Winter's insides melted. Though she hadn't been anywhere near her grandmother's closet, someone else clearly had. She wasn't sure what to say without making her grandmother worry about someone going through her home.

Noah snatched the phone from her hand. "I took them, Beth. I wanted some pictures of Winter when she was small. Something to make a nice collection for our bedroom. Pictures of us as kids. Wanted to do that for our wedding, but never got the chance." Noah winked at Winter. "I thought I told you."

She wanted to kiss her husband for taking control of the situation. She should've come up with something like that to appease her grandmother, but Winter wasn't the interior decorating type, and Gramma Beth would've known that. Hell, she still hadn't finished unpacking from their move.

"Oh, that's fine, then." Gramma Beth's upbeat voice filled the living room. "I want to see that when you're done, Noah. It'll be lovely to look at your childhood pictures. I bet you were a handful as a little boy."

Noah's laughed might've sounded genuine to Beth, but Winter recognized his concern.

"Tell Winter to call me tomorrow with a time Kline can come by. I didn't want those damn safety rails, but now my doctor is pestering the life out of me to get them."

"Bethie, stop complaining and just admit you've warmed up to the idea of having something extra in the bathroom for both of us."

Winter didn't bother to try and referee the dispute between her grandparents. Her mind was still focused on who had broken into her family's home. *And where the hell is Kline?*

"I'll tell Winter to call you tomorrow." Noah spoke clearly so Jack could hear as well. "And Jack's right. You need the safety rails, Beth."

"See? He agrees with me."

"Oh, hush, you ole blabbermouth." Her grandmother hung up before Noah could tell her goodbye.

Winter took the phone from his hands, ensuring the call had disconnected before she spoke. "What the hell? Someone was in their house stealing pictures of me?"

Noah placed his hands on her shoulders. "Maybe Beth misplaced them. You know she hasn't been well, and her memory's been off since she's been sick. Don't jump to conclusions."

As Winter pulled away from him, she tossed her phone onto the sofa. "Cameras, spyware on my computers, and missing pictures of me. This isn't a competitor or a past case. It has to either be the killer or someone in Justin's crowd. Or perhaps both at the same time?"

Noah just looked at her. They'd covered this line of thinking already, so there was nothing for him to say.

She wiped her brow, taking some comfort in the fact that her brother's incarceration had remained as stringent as the law would allow. "Who's doing this? It'd have to be someone close to me. Someone who could keep an eye on me."

"And who's close to you? Who's had access to your computers at your office and your grandparents' home?"

In her head, she sifted through the list of suspects, her stomach dropping when one particular name stood out. "Kline didn't show up at the office before. He's had access to every part of my life."

Noah nodded. "That would explain a lot about why he's been sticking close to you."

Winter put her hand to her mouth, recalling the text. "He left me a note under the door about meeting someone for breakfast, then he sent a text saying he had to help a friend and wouldn't be in the office. But the man doesn't have any friends. He's always made a point of telling me that. So why send me such a text? And why blow off Gramma?"

Noah pursed his lips. "Unless it wasn't him. He's attached to that app." He retrieved her phone from the sofa. "Call him."

She waited as the number rang. After the voicemail picked up, she redialed Kline's number.

The second time the voicemail answered, she held her phone out to Noah. "Goes to voicemail. Four times so far today." She lowered her head. "We'd agreed he'd use the app but only on my tablet, and only during certain times of the day. And never from his home IP address."

"And did he stick to your rules?"

"Actually, he responded to someone this morning when I was waiting for you outside Firebomb, and I reprimanded him. What if the killer tracked him down? It was Morninglory...no...Morningstar."

"What did he say?"

"I don't know. I went to check, but someone had deleted the messages."

"So we go to his house. But what do we tell him if he *is* home and everything's fine?"

Winter's inner alarm bells went off. "We'll start by asking why he's using the app on his phone instead of at my office like we'd agreed."

"Do you have his address?"

Winter dashed for her messenger bag by the front door, pulled out her laptop, and opened it. She sat on the sofa while sifting through the work orders she kept on her business. "I have his address under my work records. He gave it to me when he first started."

Noah hovered over her shoulder, watching her open file

after file. When she landed on the page with Kline's payment and work information, he pointed at the screen. "Fairview Apartments, number two nineteen. I know the area. It's not far." He closed Winter's laptop. "I'll drive."

"Should I call Darnell to meet us there?"

He took her hand, pulling her off the sofa as she let her laptop slide onto the cushion beside her. "Let's just see what we find when we get there. Maybe he's not answering his phone because he's asleep."

By the door, Winter reached for her jacket with trembling hands. "You really think he could be asleep at five in the afternoon?"

Noah grabbed his keys from the entryway table and opened the front door. "I sure hope so."

34

The panic creating a knot in Winter's throat hadn't let up since they started their journey to Kline's apartment. At the run-of-the-mill complex that spanned several acres, she climbed the stairs to the second floor, berating herself. She should've pieced the clues together earlier and prevented the possibility of anyone she knew getting hurt. She wasn't about to let another killer get the upper hand.

Unfortunately, there were limits to her abilities. She was one person working alone, not an agent with a team around her to offset her oversights. Having backup was one of the things she missed about the Bureau. Someone was always there to catch you if you screwed up.

In her new profession, she took the fall for every mishap. She needed to work harder to close this case and get to the bottom of the surveillance haunting her life. Those were the priorities.

She hurried along a faintly lit hall, where the black numbers of the apartments stood out against the peach-colored doors. She hadn't pictured Kline living in such a generic place. She pictured him as a *cottage outside of town* type who kept several feral cats fed. Apartment living wasn't his style.

Her sigh circled the air when she discovered the number *219* on the door. Winter knocked furiously, praying her loyal contractor would be inside.

She stopped and waited, but no one answered.

Winter knocked again, harder than before.

Again, silence greeted her.

"Shit." She punched the door. "Something's wrong."

Noah grasped her hand and carefully inspected her fingers for injury. When he was done, he let her go. "Stay here. I'll get a super to open the apartment for us."

"How?" She rubbed her aching knuckles.

He grinned. "My badge."

Noah raced down the hallway. Winter thanked providence she'd married him. Every day, the small things he did strengthened her love for him. He was always there, always watching out for her.

When she glanced at the door and thought of the older man who'd come into her life, her guilt resurfaced. Who watched out for Kline? If they found him safe and unharmed, Winter vowed to make more of an effort to show the man he wasn't alone.

And if he's not alive?

The ugly voice in her head that always posed questions she never wanted to consider awakened her anger. Heaven help anyone who touched Kline. She wouldn't hesitate to pull that trigger.

Although she dialed his number again and again, he still didn't pick up. After an eternity of waiting, Noah returned with a very round man dressed in jeans and a heavy metal band t-shirt.

"This is Mr. Cassidy. I explained the situation, and he's going to let us in."

"I never met the guy in two nineteen." Mr. Cassidy fumbled with a key chain crowded with hundreds of keys. "I got over two hundred residents in this complex. I couldn't tell you who's who around here."

"We appreciate the help," Winter told him. "We just need to make sure Kline is safe."

"Sure, yeah." Mr. Cassidy put the key in the lock. "Anything to help the FBI."

Winter mouthed *thank you* to her husband as Mr. Cassidy unlocked the door.

"I have to wait out here while you go in." Mr. Cassidy pushed the door open. "Company rules."

Desperate for an answer regarding Kline's whereabouts, Winter busted inside the apartment.

Part of her prepared to find him on the floor, already dead. She steadied herself as she turned on an overhead light.

A lingering aroma of burnt popcorn hit her first. At least it wasn't the pungent smell of death.

That's a good sign.

The living room was almost bare except for an old sofa, a very banged-up and overturned coffee table, and a small TV resting on top of a crate. There were no pictures on the walls, no knickknacks, nothing to give a hint about the personality of the person who rented the apartment.

In the dining room, one chair was toppled on its side.

Her time at Quantico and with the Bureau had taught her to evaluate every scene, to scour for details that would tell her the why, who, what, and how of a crime.

"Are you thinking what I'm thinking?" Her voice didn't rise above a whisper as Noah came to stand alongside her.

He motioned deeper into the apartment. "Let's keep going and see what else we find."

In the kitchen, the microwave door hung open, a bag of burnt popcorn still waiting inside.

"Looks like he was popping popcorn when something happened." Noah checked over the cabinets and peered into the sink. "Nothing else seems out of place here."

"Bedroom next." Winter's voice cracked as she spoke. "Then we'll have to call someone."

Noah took her hand. "One step at a time."

The walk from the kitchen to the hall leading to the only bedroom was short, less than five feet, but it felt like forever to Winter. Seconds dragged, and sweat beaded her upper lip as she dreaded what might await them.

Noah reached the bedroom first. As he opened the door, she held back, staying in the hall, unable to move.

The lights inside the room flashed and spilled into the hallway. Winter tried to follow her husband in but couldn't. She didn't want to see her friend lying in a pool of blood.

"Winter, you need to look at this."

She forced herself to put one foot in front of the other.

Soon, she had passed the threshold. To her relief, she met with no stench of blood or decay, no spray or splatter on the walls, and no sign of Kline anywhere.

What she did find was an eerily familiar scene. A simple bed with a few articles of clothing spread on top. A nightstand.

And several old pictures taped to a wall. A collage of images of a young girl in cracked and yellowed photos. Winter didn't need to get any closer to know what those photos would reveal.

Noah waved toward the pictures, unaware of how hard Winter was working to maintain control.

The images showed her spending time with her grandparents when they lived outside of Harrisonburg, Virginia. It had been the highlight of her childhood. Her Grampa Jack had taken hundreds of photos, many of which hung before her.

Noah leaned against the wall, gauging her reaction. "Why does Kline have pictures of you on his wall?"

Winter caressed the old memories. She didn't see any showing Justin or her mother. So why would those images have appeared in her vision? Whatever the answer, Noah had asked the more pressing question, and she followed it with another.

"Do you think this means he's the Wandering Hearts killer?"

"I'm more concerned with how Kline got these photos."

Winter stood back, taking in the collage. "When he came over to my house that day, Gramma Beth was with me. She gave him her keys to take measurements in her bathroom for the safety rails her doctor wanted. He had free access to the house and plenty of time to go through it. I know we've gotten close, but this borders on obsession."

Noah held her shoulders. "Could he be behind the cameras? He had access to our house, your office, Jack and Beth's place, all of it. I'm beginning to believe Kline isn't who he says he is."

Winter scrubbed her face, feeling raw. "No, that's not a possibility. I vetted the guy. There were no red flags. You vetted the guy. No criminal past. Nothing."

"The guy was a vagabond before settling in Austin and working construction. Other than that, I found nothing on him. That doesn't mean it isn't there. Who knows why he showed up at your office in the first place?"

She spun around to face him. "Kline has been there for me. Covered my ass. Protected me. He saved me from the Electrocutioner for goodness' sake. He doesn't need cameras to watch my every move. He's with me all day at the office. This doesn't make any sense."

She shuddered at the idea that Kline could be part of a bigger scheme to bring her down. Was Justin behind his showing up at her office? Did her brother have his hooks in the contractor? The thought of working so closely with someone under her brother's influence made her physically ill.

Could I be so stupid?

Winter regrouped, still fighting to conjure a logical explanation. She redirected her attention from Noah to the room around her. There had to be more to learn about Kline from where he lived.

She studied his unmade trundle bed, as well as the nightstand next to it and the clothes piled atop a chair. He had no dresser or other furniture.

Approaching the closet, she flung open the door. Inside, she found only jeans, more overalls, and a perfectly pressed blue suit. While the suit was dated and likely hadn't seen the light of day in years, it remained free of dust and lint.

"You know what he doesn't have," Noah said behind her, "is a computer. I haven't spotted one in the apartment."

Winter closed the closet door. "Kline hates technology. He barely knows how to use his phone."

Noah cocked an eyebrow. "We haven't found that either. I figured it might be here, seeing as how he hasn't answered your calls all day."

Winter lifted her own phone, still tightly clutched in her hand, and dialed Kline's number yet again.

While the ringing came over her speaker, she listened for any type of ringtone in the apartment. Silence.

"Wherever Kline is, his phone could be with him." Winter hurried over to Noah. "Can we get a trace on his phone?"

Noah shook his head. "Going through the legal channels at the Bureau would take more time than we have."

"Everything all right in there?" Mr. Cassidy called from the hall.

"We have to find out what happened." Noah moved to the

bedroom door. "Kline might've gotten himself in trouble with the killer. Because he's still on the app, he could still be a target. We need to find him before we can figure out why he came into your life."

Winter rested against the doorframe. "He had access to the app. It's the killer. Kline's either dead or he's been kidnapped. That has to be it."

"How do you know?"

"I saw this room, Noah. These pictures all over the wall. All of this. I had a vision this morning at my office, after I got that weird text from Kline about him having a friend."

Noah met her eyes. "We'll find him, but we need to call Darnell. It's time we brought the police in."

35

That knife was proving to be quite trustworthy. I stood over the old man I'd coaxed into the middle of the barn, having tied his ankles with the same rope I'd used on his wrists earlier. He might've been a contractor, with a grip strengthened from years of building and construction work, but he'd still never be able to break free.

I'll be the one liberating him...from life. Once I've taken care of Winter Black.

Poor Kline. He'd obviously lived a long life, even if I had my doubts about how good it had been. But he still had to die. He'd seen my face when I arrived at his apartment after he'd messaged me again early this morning. I was still coming down from the high of killing Miranda and there was "Grizzly Bear," asking if I wanted to meet for coffee.

My IP tracker showed me his location, and I had no trouble figuring out which unit belonged to him. A friendly twentysomething neighbor was perfectly happy to direct me to where "that nice older man" lived.

Kline had been so surprised once he opened the door and saw me standing there. He staggered back a step, making it that much easier for me to walk in, close the door behind me, and show him my knife.

He'd lifted a chair to throw at me. After I told him Winter was in danger if he didn't do as I said, he dropped the chair and demanded I take him to her. He even let me tie his hands and lead him to my car, which I'd left in a secluded part of the parking lot. The storm coming in kept the night dark enough that I didn't worry about anybody seeing us.

Once I had him in the trunk, gagged and bound, I went back into his apartment and got a measure of the man I was abducting. I needed to understand who he was, and what Winter truly meant to him.

Finding a veritable shrine of photographs featuring Winter's childhood on his bedroom wall wasn't what I'd expected, but the discovery gave me a little to go on. And I'd pull the rest out of him soon.

Ever since I'd staked out Winter and Noah's ridiculous attempted sting at Peek-a-Brew, I'd known for a fact that I would have to kill her. My fury at being treated like some common criminal nearly put me over the edge.

I'd almost dashed across the street to thrust my knife into Winter's chest. But her husband, the FBI agent, had stood up. I didn't know if he'd seen me or not, but I couldn't risk it, so I'd left as quickly as I could.

The blond wig I wore that day ended up in the nearest dumpster.

Now here I am in an old barn with an old man tied up and expecting me to kill him. I might, but first we need to have a little chat.

Taking Kline hadn't been part of my initial plan, but he was a cheater too. Not the kind I'd been targeting so far, but a liar and deceiver just the same.

A few minutes spent digging through city records and other information online gave me all the proof I needed. The

real Kline Hurst looked nothing like the man on the floor.
The man I'd traced from Winter Black's office back to his
apartment—where he'd been messaging me on Wandering
Hearts—was a mystery indeed.

We would talk, and I would learn what he was *really*
doing for Winter Black, and why he cared so much about
her. Then he would die, and no one would find him.

I ripped the gag from his mouth and yanked it over his
chin. "Okay, 'Kline.' Time for twenty questions."

He gurgled, spit on the dirt, and lifted his face up to glare
at me.

I sat on an upturned bucket a few feet away, watching
him watch me.

"Why'd you bring me here?"

His voice sounded hoarse. I'd offer him water, but I didn't
see the point.

"You already know who I am. You sent me messages. You
invited me to meet you." I held up his phone, which I'd
grabbed from his bedside table, and motioned to the barn
around us. "So here we are."

"I invited you to meet me, and you lied. You said Winter
was in danger, but really, you're just using me to put her in
danger. Aren't you?"

"Oh, Kline." He sounded so angry. Not the stance to take
with someone wielding a knife who had you bound in the
middle of nowhere. "I've seen your little shrine to Winter
Black. Why do you care so much about her?"

"If you've seen those photographs, then you know the
truth."

"I saw those pictures of Winter on your wall, but that
only tells me you're fascinated by her or obsessed. Who is she
to you?"

Coughing, he spit on the ground again. "That's none of
your business."

I liked his spirit. "So if you're not stalking her for sex, then why the obsession?" I scratched my chin. "Could she be something more to you?"

Kline's eyes disappeared as his brow wrinkled. "I have no idea what you're talking about."

"Yes, you do. Why else would you work as a contractor? And under an assumed name, no less." I adjusted my ass on the bucket. "I just want to know why you care so much, why she's gracing your walls."

My captive's face relaxed, and his glare grew colder. "I'm not saying anything to a psychotic killer. How many people have you hurt to soothe some twisted obsession of your own?"

In that moment, he reminded me of Simon. My ex-boyfriend was always so quick to label my interests as obsessions.

Who the hell did this old sack of lies think he was talking to?

Standing up, I approached him, letting him see the blade in my hand.

He put on a brave face, trying to conceal his fear, but I saw the truth. Terror danced in his blue eyes like sunlight on the water. You only had to see it once to remember it for a lifetime.

I stooped, inching close to his face while his gaze followed my every move.

I lowered the blade to his crotch. "Now I'll ask you again, and you should think carefully about what answer you're going to give me. Who is Winter Black to you?"

36

Winter paced Darnell's office. She kept looking back at the dark-eyed detective, praying he'd help locate her contractor.

"And you're sure this man isn't just mad at you and refusing to take your calls?" Darnell's sigh stretched across the room. "*I'd* ignore you if I could."

Noah stood in front of the detective's desk, glaring down at him. "Kline's not answering his phone, there were signs of a struggle at his apartment, and there's that weird picture thing of Winter on his wall. We came to you first thing."

Darnell rubbed his finger along his temple. "Yeah, I get that. But how do you know he's missing? I can't do much of anything. As an adult, he can disappear for a while if he wants. Tell me why we should put out a Clear Alert for the man."

Winter stopped pacing. "Because I created a profile on Wandering Hearts using some of his information, with the aim of enticing the killer. I did it for both my employees, with their consent, to try and get a lead."

Darnell rocked forward in his chair. "You did what?"

Winter ignored the fury in his voice. "I had control over

the messages they received in the beginning, but then Kline convinced me I didn't come across as a man, and he took over his account. I know he signed onto the app and communicated with someone, but the messages were wiped clean afterward. It has to be our killer's doing. He was on the app, and now he's missing. This isn't a coincidence. The last four murders should prove that."

Darnell aimed his finger at her. "You of all people should know better than to put civilians in danger."

Noah moved to stand next to his wife. "I went along with it. I believed she might get more responses using her office staff because they came across as more genuine than any agent we'd put up on the app."

Darnell stood, banging his fist on the desk. "You two are working in tandem to drive me crazy. Seriously, you know better, Dalton. This is an FBI investigation now. You could've put your badge on the line."

Winter stepped in front of her husband. "It's all me. It's my fault. Lock me up, press charges—do whatever the hell you want—but please help us find Kline."

With his hands on his hips, Darnell glared at the two of them. "Why should I compromise my job by helping you?"

Winter approached the detective's desk. "Because I made contact. I was supposed to meet someone at a local café, and they never showed, but I did see a tall blond woman all but run from the coffee shop across the street. I think that was the killer, and we spooked them. Then this happens with Kline. The killer must know who I am and what I was doing. I think this has gotten personal."

Darnell returned to his chair and straightened his jacket sleeves. He picked up a pen and cleared his throat. "Okay. I'll play along. Did you ever see anyone suspicious hanging around your office? Any strange or unusual occurrences?"

Winter hesitated. If she told Darnell everything, the man

would never speak to her again, but if she didn't, Kline might end up dead before she or anyone else could save him.

"There's spyware loaded on my work computers. Someone was watching us. My assistant found it by running scans, but when we went in search of a program, nothing was in the hard drive. That's why I think they went after Kline. They'd been watching us. They knew we were onto them."

Darnell sat back. "And you have no idea who this might be?"

Winter shook her head. "No. I haven't seen anyone around the office or our home. I wish I had more, but I don't."

Darnell said nothing for the longest time. Winter worried he might haul her off to jail—or at least try and get her investigator's license revoked.

"You said you saw a tall blond woman the day you were supposed to meet someone from the app?"

"That's right. I'm not sure I could give you more information than that or pick anyone out of a lineup, though. I remember a solid-looking build, long legs, and definitely a woman's figure."

He tapped his chin. "Let me show you something, see if you can pick out this tall woman for me." Darnell turned to his computer.

He typed something as Winter waited. She glanced at Noah, wondering if he had any idea what Darnell had, but he appeared just as clueless.

Darnell swung the monitor of his computer around to face her. "We got the surveillance tapes from the night Miranda Freeman was killed at the Firebomb. We were lucky they had separate surveillance on the second floor by their office."

A grainy image appeared on the screen. While dark,

Winter could make out the sconces she remembered from the nightclub's second floor.

"These are from about an hour before Miranda arrived. There are several people heading to the upstairs VIP lounge, so watch closely. See if you recognize anyone."

After Darnell finished with his instructions, she hunched closer to the desk, resting her elbows on the surface as the images flicked across the screen.

Faces were hard to make out, and she could only get wispy images of a few of the people when they stopped below the sconces. She tensed as she watched the video, checking the time clock on the bottom left.

"The time Miranda arrived at the club is coming up." Darnell pointed at the screen. "She'll come out of the left corner."

Almost on cue, Winter spotted her. The stunning woman she'd only remembered as a decaying corpse appeared vibrant, with so much of her life ahead of her. She glided along the hall, heading toward the arched doorway at the end. Before she reached the private balcony for VIPs, she stepped out of frame.

Winter peered over the top of the computer. "I didn't see anyone. Nightclub lighting doesn't exactly make it easy to pick out faces."

"Keep an eye on the screen. What you're seeing now is the video at about the time of Miranda Freeman's murder." Darnell's voice became a whisper. "A few more people come and go at this point, then the light changes."

Winter paid close attention. She saw more of the same— shadowed faces that rapidly blurred as the people moved across the camera's view. A strobing light illuminated the area and nearly every figure began squirming where they stood. "Music must've changed. That strobe light's new."

"Uh-huh. DJ puts it on when he's playing a hot dance tune. We got that from the club owners. Keep watching."

The strobe continued to wash over the figures of men and women, until it landed on one very familiar face before sweeping away.

"Go back. Rewind about three seconds and slow the video down."

As the image froze, Winter waited, chewing her bottom lip and praying her eyes hadn't deceived her.

The video restarted, and there was the woman Winter had met at the jewelry store. Her hair hung about her shoulders, and she wore a black getup that Winter couldn't decipher, but her face stood out clearly in the light.

"I know her." She glanced over at Noah. "That's the woman I interviewed at All Is Gold. It's an upscale jewelry store."

Darnell came around the desk to her side. "I have two detectives checking the jewelry stores too. Looking for that charm, right?"

Still staring at Cassie's frozen face on the screen, Winter nodded. "I went to find out more about the charms. She helped me. Her name is Cassie Pattell. I remember her because she seemed to think the charm was the kind of cheap trinket you'd get at one of those junky party favor stores."

Darnell swiveled the monitor around as he sat back down in his desk chair. "Cassie Pattell? Let me get an address." He typed at his keyboard and waited before pumping a fist in the air.

"Got her driver's license. She's over on Haddock Street. Not far from here."

Winter moved toward the office door. "Great. Let's go to her place and ask her if she knows anything."

"No." Darnell picked up his office phone. "We're going by the book on this one. I'm going to bring her in for questioning. We can go over and pick her up without a warrant since she's a person of interest from this point on."

"What about Kline?"

"The fifty-something adult male who isn't answering his phone? Look, I'll put out an APB, just in case. That's all I can do right now. If we find anything incriminating at this Pattell woman's place, we'll go from there. And thank you for your help. I mean that."

"I know you do, but I'm hoping this isn't a brush-off. I want to be at Pattell's. If she's the killer, she'll recognize me and know I've helped you catch her. That might compel her to reveal what she knows about Kline."

"Assuming there's something to know." He threw up his hands in surrender. "I'm not brushing you off. Yes, you can come along. Just know, this is my rodeo."

Winter nudged Noah, and they traded a look. They'd stay in their lane and let Darnell lead the interview—assuming Pattell was even at home and available to *be* interviewed.

If she isn't, and if that's because she's taken Kline somewhere to kill him, then she'd better know a really good hiding place. Because I'm done letting killers dictate my moves.

37

After a long, frustrating drive through dark, rain-slicked streets, Noah and Winter finally followed Darnell down Haddock Road in Noah's truck. The area was filled with blocks of apartments, but unlike where Kline lived, Noah knew these complexes boasted luxury units and condos with private gardens and rolling rivers cutting through parklike grounds. He'd driven past the exclusive community many times on his way to the FBI building. He'd often wondered what hid behind the high gates.

Now he'd get his chance to find out.

The guard who escorted them from the front gate to Cassie Pattell's building had almost fainted when Darnell flashed his badge and demanded to speak with one of the neighborhood's residents.

"It's a matter of life and death," the detective had said.

At the time, Noah had wanted to laugh, thinking that was only a line used by cops on TV.

The guard only agreed to show them through the complex after a supervisor insisted their group could not be let loose without a representative of the building management accompanying them.

Even in the cover of a stormy night, the landscaping shocked Noah. They went through a long courtyard featuring lavish ponds and fountains, lush green ferns, and crepe myrtle trees.

"Are you thinking what I'm thinking?" Winter pulled her jacket hood tighter against the slanting rain.

"Yeah. Why can't we live here?"

Winter nudged his ribs. "No. How can Cassie Pattell, a salesperson in a jewelry shop, afford such a place? One of the other shop attendants I interviewed made a comment about his ex dating someone who 'earns more than jewelry counter wages.' This is high-end living, Noah. Big money."

Noah shifted his focus back to the case. "Yeah, *not buying a political appointment* big, but still high dollar. You thinking she does something illicit on the side? Maybe jewelry smuggling?"

Before Winter could reply, their security guard escort motioned to a building up ahead. "She lives in the Dumaine Building."

Noah eyed the structure. "Dumaine? Why Dumaine?"

The guard waved at the courtyard surrounding them. "Every building is named after a street in the French Quarter of New Orleans. The builders wanted to recreate the atmosphere, but they left out the one thing that makes that place special. The bars."

He ushered them into a breezeway, then through a door to a bank of elevators. Noah was grateful for the reprieve from the rain. He let Darnell and Winter get in first, then joined them for the ride up to the third floor, where Cassie Pattell's apartment was located.

"Does Miss Pattell live alone?" Darnell asked the guard.

He shrugged his wide shoulders. "Got me. I don't talk to

her much. She keeps to herself a lot. Never says more than a few words when she comes and goes through the gate."

When they arrived on her floor and the guard led them to her door, Noah instinctively reached for his gun. He had to chuckle to himself when his hand felt nothing on his belt. He'd left the weapon in his truck at Darnell's insistence. It was the Austin PD bringing Pattell in for questioning. Not the FBI.

He knew his ass was already on the line, but if he cracked the case, Falkner might trust him with more field work in the future. Better that than the alternative.

I won't make a very good pastry chef.

The guard stopped at a door with the letter *D* boldly painted in black. "This is her."

Darnell moved to the front of the group. "I'll take it from here." He rapped lightly on the door. "Miss Pattell, this is Detective Davenport with the Austin Police Department. I need to speak with you."

Noah kept his ear close to the door, alert to any possible rustling or movement from within. If Cassie Pattell was involved in this whole Wandering Hearts affair, she might use this opportunity to bolt.

He waited, but other than the patter of rain on the ground outside, they might as well have been in a church. Then he aimed a thumb at the door. "Seems like no one's home."

Darnell knocked again, with more force than before.

Noah heard nothing coming from inside the apartment.

Darnell spun toward the guard. "You got a master key, yes? We need to get in and make sure she's okay. I may have heard someone whimpering inside." He traded a quick conspiratorial look with Noah.

Nodding, the guard reached for a key chain on his belt. "Yeah, hold on."

Noah's anticipation tickled his insides as the guard opened the door.

When a whoosh of air from inside wafted into the hallway, caressing Noah's cheeks, he detected the slightest essence of honeysuckle.

The guard stood by the threshold and waved Darnell in. "It's all yours. I'm supposed to stay out here until you find something."

"Let's hope we don't find anything." Darnell directed his next words through the open door. "This is Detective Davenport, Austin PD. Does anyone inside require assistance? I'm coming in."

Noah entered before Winter, wanting to protect her from any traps or horrific sights that might await them. He knew it was unnecessary. She'd seen more than him in the field, but, as she was his wife and his world, he still felt that overwhelming desire to protect her at all costs. If he could spare her any pain, then he would do his utmost to shield her.

The spacious apartment boasted muted tones of brown and taupe furniture in the living area. Paintings of colorful woods with bubbling brooks adorned the walls. Noah stepped closer to one of the pictures, amazed to discover it wasn't a print. He could see the brushstrokes on the canvas.

"Bet that wasn't cheap." Winter stood next to him, studying the portrait. "This woman has expensive taste."

"Guys?" Darnell's voice echoed across the enormous living room.

Following the sound, Noah found the man in an alcove. Inside the space, a rectangular table held four different computers, each running a program as their screens scrolled through pages and pages of data.

"Holy shit." Noah approached the computer closest to him. "You said this woman worked in a jewelry store."

Winter lifted a box of burner phones from the table. "By the looks of this operation, the jewelry store's the side hustle."

"I'll check out the rest of the place." Darnell slipped away, his gun gripped in his hand.

"You see this?" After pulling on a glove, Winter pressed the space bar on the computer farthest from Noah. "It's logged into Wandering Hearts."

He checked the screen and saw a host of private DMs rolling in from the app. He read a few of the messages, each addressed to a different person. "She must have dozens of identities she's running through a shadow system. Something that monitors the app from different routers."

Winter bent and glanced under the table. "Like these?"

Noah knelt down for a better view. Below the table were four different routers. Each hooked up to a different computer. It was one of those *aha* moments Noah relished on a case. When the clues came together, he got a peek inside the mind of a criminal. In this case, the mind of a killer.

"I don't think this is a coincidence. Cassie Pattell is definitely involved in this case. Either she's our killer or she's working with them."

Darnell returned to the alcove. "The rest of the apartment's clear. I'm gonna call the station to get a team down here to collect all this stuff."

Noah scanned the hardware on the table, astounded by the setup. "We're dealing with someone skilled in computer programming. It would explain why Cyber had a tough time chasing down IP addresses for the app host."

"So any idea where our girl is?" Darnell put his gun back in his shoulder holster.

Winter gazed at the open door to the hall. "Maybe we should check with some neighbors. See if anyone has spoken to her lately."

Darnell removed his phone from his pocket. "You two stay here while I call this in. Let me handle the neighbors."

Noah glanced at his wife. "You had no idea when you talked to this woman?"

Winter let out a long breath as she continued to eye the table covered with computer equipment. "Nothing stood out. She was as normal as every other salesperson I talked to."

"If she's the killer, she's got a hell of an operation here. Who's to say she's never done this before in another state?" He ran his hand over his hair. "I've never seen anything like this in a murder investigation. Money laundering or a gambling ring maybe, but this is intricate."

Winter wrapped her arms around her chest. "Makes you wonder what happened to her. How someone talented enough to pull this off could end up killing people."

"If she killed them," Noah corrected. "We only have the video linking her to one crime."

"And Kline? Where is he?"

The fear in her voice gutted him. He'd never heard his wife so afraid. He'd heard her angry, sad, happy, and ecstatic, but this was an emotion she rarely showed anyone.

He put his arm around her, wishing he could take away her pain. He knew Winter, and whenever anyone she cared about was in trouble, she blamed herself. She felt her gift should save everyone she loved, but it didn't work that way, and there were days he'd seen her torn apart by her past and the suffering she'd survived.

Noah knew the best help he could offer was to be there and listen. He tried to always be available. Sometimes, their clashing schedules made that difficult. But for right now, right here, he had to be her rock.

Darnell hurried back through the door. "I've got something. The neighbor next door stopped me in the hall.

She was curious about what was going on. She says Cassie spends a lot of time at her family's farm outside the city."

Winter walked to a mantle above the gas fireplace, where she browsed the framed picture collection before selecting one of the black-and-white photos.

"Is this it?" She carried the picture back to Noah.

An old photo with yellowed edges showed a young girl with long, flowing, wavy hair holding a small chick in her hands. Two smokestacks rose in the distance behind her head, and a proud, happy smile painted her face. Noah couldn't imagine this young girl as the same person who'd callously stabbed four people to death. But people grew up. And people changed.

Darnell took the picture from Winter. "I know where this is. Off highway twenty-nine, there's an old brewery. You see the smokestacks in the background? The buildings are still standing, but they've been abandoned for years. We get bodies being dropped out that way a lot. Cartel kills mostly. Mules that made a run for it instead of paying up. There're farms all around."

"Then that's where we have to go." Winter raised her eyes to Noah. "Kline might be there."

Darnell touched Winter's arm. "This woman next door thought we were here to help. She said, 'Cassie's not been right since her boyfriend left her.'"

Noah knew they'd gotten their woman. Now all they had to do was catch her and hand her over to the courts.

"Call the Bureau before you go." Darnell directed a hard gaze at him. "If you don't alert them about this, it'll be your ass."

Darnell was right. No matter how much Noah wanted to lie low, his duty was to report the discovery.

"No, we can't wait for agents and officers to catalogue the

scene." Winter sounded frantic. "Kline might be in danger. We have to go."

Noah glanced at Darnell, knowing he had no choice but to go with his wife.

Darnell conceded with a nod. "Go, both of you. I'll cover everything with your people. Once the forensic team arrives, I'll join you at the farm."

In that instant, Noah's opinion of Darnell changed. He'd survived one precarious situation at the Magic Carpet Dry Cleaning warehouse with the detective, and now, he knew he could trust him. Darnell had been there for Winter, and Noah was certain he'd be there for him as well.

Besides, Noah wasn't about to let Winter head out to the farm alone. His job wasn't worth having if it meant putting his wife in danger. He could finally feel useful and do something instead of sitting behind a desk, staring at a computer screen.

"Just be careful." Darnell seemed to direct his warning mostly at Winter. "I've got enough dead bodies associated with this case. I don't want any more."

Noah guided Winter out of the apartment with no intention of becoming a statistic. He had his entire life with Winter to look forward to, and he wasn't going to let a homicidal maniac ruin his plans.

38

Kline rolled his head from left to right and back again, attempting to work out the kink building up from having lain on the barn floor for so long. He heard rain pelting the roof above. A steady drip was forming a small puddle down by his feet.

It was so dark, he guessed it had to be nighttime, but he'd lost track of the hours she'd kept him tied up to a post in the blackest corner of the barn. He vaguely recalled being dragged through musty straw and dirt and shoved against the wood.

His back hurt, his muscles shook, and he was sick of the stench of musty hay and flies buzzing around him. The stains and wrinkles on his overalls testified to his ordeal.

But he'd seen worse in his days.

Done worse too. You know it, old man. You've earned this, same as every other sinner on Earth.

His desire to finally reveal himself to the people who mattered was the only thing that kept him going.

He'd worked hard to get his life together. He was so near to becoming the man he'd longed to be. Kline didn't want everything to end in an old run-down barn. It wasn't fair. The car accident had been a wake-up call. One he had heeded. And he'd turned his life around, vowing to uphold the name of the dead man he'd killed.

He'd heard about Justin Black, and he knew about the horrible things The Preacher had done to the boy—and to Winter. If Kline had been there, would the past have been any different?

Probably not, you sad old drunk.

The night he learned about what happened to Winter's family, Kline had gone out and gotten so wasted he could hardly walk straight, much less drive a car.

He'd seen the homeless man stumbling alongside the road, but he hadn't slowed. The world outside the windshield seemed fake, like a television screen instead of a window. Hypnotized, he watched the man spin around in the headlights and throw his hands up. Kline, realizing too late that the man was actually in front of him, swerved and lost his grip on the wheel.

The next thing he remembered was waking up slumped over the wheel with the car in a ditch and a dying man sprawled across the hood.

His license had already been suspended, and Kline knew this crime would guarantee he'd spend the rest of his days behind bars. He wasn't willing to do that.

So he held the hand of the man he'd hit, waiting for him to die. The moment he'd breathed his last, Kline had traded identities with him. John Drewitt had died on the side of the road that night, and Kline Hurst had survived.

No one would care about the death of the screwup John Drewitt. A gambler, liar, drunkard, and cheat, Drewitt had wasted his life until killing a man had sobered him up. He didn't want to be who he was, so he became the dead man instead.

After disposing of the body in the middle of nowhere, he'd assumed Kline's identity. The dead man had no one. No family, no home. He'd been practically invisible, and from what Drewitt could figure, homeless for years.

Posing as Kline, he'd picked up jobs in construction. It was a line of work he'd known well from his teenage years and one where no one checked references. If you could swing a hammer, you were good.

A few jobs got him references, and he became established. It wasn't until after he'd assumed the dead man's identity that he considered his sister. Opal was all he had left in the world, and losing her only family would've devastated her. John couldn't bear that.

He'd contacted Opal and told her what happened. She buried the man he'd killed in the family plot and kept his secret—a feat, considering how awful Opal was with secrets. Her support had kept him going through the years.

Now he was back in the same precarious life he'd walked away from, but not by his own doing. By Winter's.

He couldn't let her down. He couldn't let the killer win. He had to get out of this mess for her. Winter was all that mattered to him at this point.

As his captor approached, Kline decided the time had come to reason with her. Talk to her and buy time until he could free himself and get help.

"Where are we?"

She squatted beside him. "My family's old barn. I grew up here. It's the Double Bar Farm, not far from Austin." She held out a water bottle and let a trickle fall into Kline's mouth, which he greedily lapped at, even as most of it spilled down his chin.

Chuckling, she pulled the bottle away, exacerbating his torturous ache for water. "You're probably wondering why. All my victims wonder that."

Kline licked his lips, reminding himself to not show his anger. "Actually, I was asking myself what had driven you to this point in your life. It had to be someone who lied to you or hurt you. People aren't naturally born with so much villainy."

She stood again, clutching the bottle. Her mouth opened as if she were about to speak, but she remained silent. Kline could feel the confusion seeping from her bones.

"His name was Simon Chen." Sadness tinged her voice. "I met him in college. He was from Taiwan, and we talked about how we would return to his family's home and start our life together. Then, one day, he was gone. He stole something I helped him build and sold it. He got all the glory and all the money. Then he dumped me and left for Taiwan with another coworker, who I later found out he'd been engaged to all along. I read about their upcoming nuptials on the internet. I wanted so badly to make sure he never saw his bride walk down the aisle."

Kline concentrated on his facial muscles, striving to keep any hint of judgment hidden. "I lost someone once. She made me happy, and then she left. I never found her again."

She leaned toward him, an inkling of trust emanating from her. "Then you understand what I'm doing. Those who cheat must pay. We can't let people who willingly hurt others continue to live. Imagine all the broken hearts I'm saving."

"But you're still breaking hearts. Your murders revealed the secrets the dead hoped to hide. Their loved ones still suffer. Now they have to overcome the cheating *and* the loss. You didn't fix anything. Heartbreak isn't a reason to kill."

She tossed the water bottle onto a pile of old hay, far out of his reach. Then she retrieved the knife she'd set aside and brought the blade to within inches of Kline's face.

"What the hell do you know? I saw your pitiful apartment and that display on your wall of Winter. Does she know how you feel about her? I bet not. So don't sit there and tell me about loss. You wallow in yours. I've done something about mine."

As she raised the knife, he reflexively lifted his bound hands to stave off the blow.

When the knife punctured his right hand, he howled.

She yanked the blade out, adding to his misery. The horrible sound of bone and sinew tearing made him want to vomit.

Blood gushed from the wound, spilling down his overalls. Images of his work in repairs flashed before his eyes. What if he couldn't hold a hammer or pinch a nail? He'd be worthless. The potential loss of livelihood compounded the searing agony.

He rolled to his side, fighting back the tears. He couldn't give her the satisfaction of seeing him break down.

The woman stood over him, brandishing the knife still dripping in his blood and looking as if she wanted to drive the blade into his chest.

As he stared up at her, the sheer villainy and hatred pouring from her radiated like hellfire. She wore the same black clothes she'd had on when she arrived at his apartment. Her triumphant laugh came to his ears like crackling flames as she stepped away to vanish into the darkness of the barn.

Not since the night he'd killed the real Kline Hurst had he been so afraid. He was once again the pathetic John Drewitt, praying for the strength to deal with his mistakes. He'd made a deadly one when deciding to take on the Wandering Hearts killer.

He'd intended to spare Winter any danger, but his plan had backfired. Now he might end up like the man he'd murdered—killed and forgotten.

His sins had finally caught up to him.

39

The bumpy road tossed Winter around in the cab of Noah's large truck as she peered out the window, searching for the smokestacks of the abandoned brewery. The rain had slowed but continued to fall in a steady drizzle. All she could see were the silhouettes of trees and the occasional glow of lights from a farmhouse.

Winter's mind bounced from thoughts of stopping Cassie to saving Kline. She couldn't help but blame herself for his capture. It had been her plan to use him and Ariel to lure the killer. She'd never intended for the ploy to go this far.

"He'll be fine." Noah maneuvered the road from the highway.

In the distance, something rose from the dark line of trees. Her heart quickened. "There. See it? Right ahead. Is that a smokestack?"

Noah hit the gas. "It sure is."

The road they followed came to an abrupt dead end. Fields of green surrounded them on both sides while the smokestacks billowed up like black pillars in the background.

The scene was very similar to the picture Winter had seen on Cassie's mantel. Even the trees along the road appeared familiar. Taller, but definitely the same oaks.

She got out of the truck and left her jacket hood down, allowing the drizzle to fall on her head as she scoured the landscape for any sign of a structure. She spotted something through the trees.

"Over there." She headed toward the bulky, shadowed form.

"Wait." Noah dashed up to her. "We go together."

She was in such a rush to find Kline, to make sure he was alive, that all procedure for walking into a potential crime scene had left her. All that mattered was getting the contractor back into the fold so she could ask him what he was doing with all those pictures on his wall.

They followed a dirt path, their guns held in low-ready positions.

A heavily weathered white clapboard farmhouse appeared. Run-down and surrounded by weeds, it looked as if no one had lived there for ages.

Noah motioned to her, grabbing her attention. He put his finger over her lips, suggesting they go silent from here on out. Then he nodded to the house and raised his gun higher, prepared for anything or anyone that might charge at them.

Winter peeked in a few of the old windows, wiping away the grime so she could see inside. Some furniture sat in what she assumed was a living room, but no lights lit the house. A pile of newspapers and a stack of wood rested by the fireplace. A backpack sat on the coffee table. Someone had been there recently. She hoped this was the home Cassie had escaped to.

A cry came from the rear of the house. Winter adjusted her aim higher and circled around the back, sticking close to the structure for cover. The cry wasn't a high-pitched scream like one would associate with a woman. That had been a man, and he was in pain.

She didn't see the barn until she cleared the rear of the small home. It was a few hundred feet from the house and set in the middle of a field with high grass.

Noah paused at her side. "Stay low. Stay quiet.'"

He went ahead of her, cutting across the field, his head sticking out of the high grass no matter how low he tried to crouch.

Winter broke out in a different direction not far from him, hoping to at least give anyone watching them from the barn two targets to track. That'd double their chances of breaching the barn before getting shot.

A woman's cackle carried across the field, sharp and villainous.

Winter stooped and ran, the high, rain-wet grass slapping against her shoulders.

She tried not to pay attention to the raindrops spattering against her face, maintaining her bead on the barn. When she was within ten feet of the doors, she cut across to join Noah.

Noah pointed to the back of the barn. *Go that way*, he mouthed. *I'll take the front.*

She nodded to confirm the plan while Noah pecked her cheek.

"Sneak in slow," he whispered against her skin. "No hero moves."

She raised her head and gave him a cynical grin.

Winking, Noah took off to the front of the barn.

As she watched him go, a heavy zing crossed her heart. This was it, Winter's gamble, placing everything on the line in hopes of a better outcome. She prayed she hadn't dragged him into a situation where either one of them would end up hurt—or dead.

40

Winter tried to make her footfalls as quiet as possible, and the rainfall had helped during their initial approach, but the cover was tapering off now. She cringed as she moved closer to the barn doors. As she thought of the killer picking up her movements and rushing to hurt Kline, agony weighed down her every step.

Focus. Take out the killer, and he will be okay.

Images of him shot or dying plagued her, and her guilt swelled. She couldn't lose him. Not when she had so many questions. What did those pictures on his wall mean? Why had he taken them?

She kept her pace slow and steady, every inch forward increasing her heart rate. She was almost there. Kline was almost free.

Winter covered the last few feet, desperately trying to catch glimpses through the cracks in the barn doors. Shards of light filtered through, but not enough to allow her to detect any movement.

A branch cracked under her feet just in front of the doors. She froze, her muscles tensing. Noah's plan to be quiet and sneak up on the killer fled from her head. Winter needed to speed up their plan. She had to end this before anything else happened to her contractor. She was going to confront the Wandering Hearts murderer head-on.

Winter waited at the barn doors, holding her breath as she analyzed the gap between the edges. There was a chain across the center on the inside, but she had enough room to squeeze through. Peering into the darkness, she caught the play of shadows against a wall of hay bales. Someone inside had situated a lamp at the back of the barn.

Perfect!

The heavy thud of footsteps approaching her location let Winter know she'd been spotted. With her finger on the trigger and a Zen-like focus developed through years of training, she pushed through the gap.

A man yelled from inside the barn. "Winter, watch out!"

Straw and hay flew into her field of vision from her left. Winter rolled to the side, away from the direction of her attacker.

A figure emerged from the shadows.

As Winter settled into a crouch, a pitchfork swatted the gun from her hands. She spun with the force of the attack and rolled away again, across the ground.

Her attacker rushed forward, pitchfork raised to skewer her. Winter dodged to her left, then slid back across the floor, letting the hay and straw provide her a slick surface. She collided with her assailant—it was Pattell, all right—and wrenched the pitchfork from her grip, pinning it against the other woman's torso.

On the other side of the barn, Noah emerged from the shadows, illuminated by the lantern light as he rushed across the hay-strewn floor.

"Get over here, Dalton!"

Shrieking, Pattell wriggled free and grabbed the handle of

the pitchfork, trying to bring the tines in line with Winter's face. A swift kick to Pattell's kneecap dropped her to the ground.

Winter tore the pitchfork from the killer's grip again and flung the weapon aside. Pattell reached for her jacket pocket and drew a knife. Waving it before her as a warning for Winter to stay back, she tried to get up. Her leg half buckled as she stood, but she kept her feet.

As Winter shifted back and forth, looking for a good opening around that knife, Pattell sliced at the air between them and flung herself at Winter.

Siezing her chance, Winter sidestepped, dodging behind the killer and wrapping her arms around Pattell's upper body in a half nelson.

Even with her arms pinned to her sides, Pattell kept trying to flick the blade around her hip to slice at Winter, who had to dance sideways to avoid the sharp edge.

"Hurry it *up*, Dalton!"

But at that moment, Noah raced up to lend his hands to the task of restraining the murderer. With a kick, he knocked the blade from Pattell's hand into the straw underfoot.

Disarmed, Pattell screamed with fury as she wrenched her body side to side, but Noah and Winter held firm.

"It's over, Cassie. It's over, and the police will be here soon."

She grunted and thrashed until the wail of sirens filtered through the barn.

From somewhere behind Winter, a familiar graveled voice called out. "Would one of you untie me before the cops arrive?"

Winter recognized the crotchety tone of her favorite contractor. Noah pulled a pair of cuffs off his belt, and they applied them to Pattell, who continued to thrash about even as Noah hauled her to her feet, holding her up to avoid further injuring her knee. Winter helped get her safely positioned against a bale of moldering hay.

The sirens grew louder, closing in on the barn, and Kline was still muttering about being set free. Winter searched the dark corners of the barn until she found him, farthest from the lantern, lying on his side against a post. His hands and feet were bound with rope.

She worked on freeing him from his bindings. He was covered in muck, and blood oozed from a wound in one hand, but he was alive.

Once she untied his wrists, Kline worked his uninjured hand, getting the circulation back. After Winter unwound the rope from his legs, she helped him onto a bale of hay by the back barn doors. She knelt at his feet and checked his wounded hand.

"How did you find me?"

"A video from the night one of the victims died gave us Cassie Pattell's identity. We went to her apartment, and that led us here."

He pulled his hand away from her grip. "And did you go to my apartment?"

"We discovered the overturned furniture, yeah. And…the photos of me." She sat back on her heels in order to watch his face. "Want to tell me why?"

Kline squinted but didn't say a word.

Winter trailed his gaze. He was searching for Noah, who was on the ground next to Pattell. She'd ceased fighting and had begun to openly cry.

Blue-and-red flashing lights danced along the side of the barn, busting in through cracks and gaps in the old wood.

Winter turned her attention back to her contractor. "What's with the photo essay to my childhood, Kline?"

He cleared his throat. "This wasn't how I pictured telling

you about me. I thought I'd have more time to get to know
you first."

Noah shouted at the police officers rushing inside the
front door of the barn.

Winter remained focused on Kline, desperate for
answers. "Why did you need more time? For what?"

Kline smiled ever so slightly before brushing her cheek
with his good hand. "Because, Winter, honey, I'm your
father."

Winter's breath caught, and her mind reeled with a
whirlwind of questions and flashes from her past. She didn't
understand.

She did not understand.

She had a father. His name was Bill Black. He raised her
until she was thirteen, and she'd grieved to the very center of
her soul when The Preacher had killed him. To consider
another man her father seemed unimaginable.

Lifting her eyes to meet Kline's, Winter studied every
inch of his face, seeing him, really seeing him, for the first
time.

Kline, his gruff manner cast aside, gazed softly back,
acting like he'd give her all the time she'd ever need to
respond.

"I have your eyes."

"Yep, you sure do."

He was about to reach for her hand when paramedics
raced over.

Winter took advantage of the distraction to move back,
stand up, and slip away to let the EMTs do their thing.
Kline's hand needed medical care, and he needed water.

As she searched for Noah in the growing throng of law
enforcement, her eyes teared up, and in an effort to clear
them, she blinked in rapid time. Her emotions were ripping
her apart.

Could any of what Kline said be true, or was his claim just a well-concocted lie? She'd heard so many in her career. His could just be another to convince her to lower her guard.

But she *did* have his eyes.

And the "gift."

They shared that too. He'd told her so during her last case, right before saving her from death by electrocution.

Winter compiled lists of things she needed to do to check out his story. She also needed to tell Noah everything she'd learned from Kline. Their eyes met.

Just as she was about to rush into his arms, her phone pinged with an incoming text.

She glanced at the screen. The sender had an unidentified account. With trepidation tightening her chest, she opened the message.

Hello, Winter. Give your Daddy a kiss from me.

The End
To be continued...

Thank you for reading.
All of the Winter Black Series books can be found on Amazon.

ACKNOWLEDGMENTS

The past few years have been a whirlwind of change, both personally and professionally, and I find myself at a loss for the right words to express my profound gratitude to those who have supported me on this remarkable journey. Yet, I am compelled to try.

To my sons, whose unwavering support has been my bedrock, granting me the time and energy to transform my darkest thoughts into words on paper. Your steadfast belief in me has never faltered, and watching each of you grow, welcoming the wonderful daughters you've brought into our family, has been a source of immense pride and joy.

Embarking on the dual role of both author and publisher has been an exhilarating, albeit challenging, adventure. Transitioning from the solitude of writing to the dynamic world of publishing has opened new horizons for me, and I'm deeply grateful for the opportunity to share my work directly with you, the readers.

I extend my heartfelt thanks to the entire team at Mary Stone Publishing, the same dedicated group who first recognized my potential as an indie author years ago. Your collective efforts, from the editors whose skillful hands have polished my words to the designers, marketers, and support staff who breathe life into these books, have been instrumental in resonating deeply with our readers. Each of you plays a crucial role in this journey, not only nurturing my growth but also ensuring that every story reaches its full potential. Your dedication, creativity, and finesse have been nothing short of invaluable.

However, my deepest gratitude is reserved for you, my beloved readers. You ventured off the beaten path of traditional publishing to embrace my work, investing your most precious asset—your time. It is my sincerest hope that this book has enriched that time, leaving you with memories that linger long after the last page is turned.

With all my love and heartfelt appreciation,

Mary

ABOUT THE AUTHOR

Nestled in the serene Blue Ridge Mountains of East Tennessee, Mary Stone crafts her stories surrounded by the natural beauty that inspires her. What was once a home filled with the lively energy of her sons has now become a peaceful writer's retreat, shared with cherished pets and the vivid characters of her imagination.

As her sons grew and welcomed wonderful daughters-in-law into the family, Mary's life entered a quieter phase, rich with opportunities for deep creative focus. In this tranquil environment, she weaves tales of courage, resilience, and intrigue, each story a testament to her evolving journey as a writer.

From childhood fears of shadowy figures under the bed to a profound understanding of humanity's real-life villains, Mary's style has been shaped by the realization that the most complex antagonists often hide in plain sight. Her writing is characterized by strong, multifaceted heroines who defy traditional roles, standing as equals among their peers in a world of suspense and danger.

Mary's career has blossomed from being a solitary author to establishing her own publishing house—a significant milestone that marks her growth in the literary world. This expansion is not just a personal achievement but a reflection of her commitment to bring thrilling and thought-provoking stories to a wider audience. As an author and publisher, Mary continues to challenge the conventions of the thriller genre, inviting readers into gripping tales filled with serial killers, astute FBI agents, and intrepid heroines who confront peril with unflinching bravery.

Each new story from Mary's pen—or her publishing house—is a pledge to captivate, thrill, and inspire, continuing the legacy of the imaginative little girl who once found wonder and mystery in the shadows.

Discover more about Mary Stone on her website.
www.authormarystone.com

facebook.com/authormarystone

x.com/MaryStoneAuthor

goodreads.com/AuthorMaryStone

bookbub.com/profile/3378576590

pinterest.com/MaryStoneAuthor

instagram.com/marystoneauthor

tiktok.com/@authormarystone

Printed in Great Britain
by Amazon